FEAR OF THE DARK

GAR ANTHONY HAYWOOD

A THOMAS·DUNNE BOOK

ST. MARTIN'S PRESS NEW YORK

MYS.

FEAR OF THE DARK
Copyright © 1988 by Gar Anthony Haywood. All rights reserved.
Printed in the United States of America. No part of this book may
be used or reproduced in any manner whatsoever without written
permission except in the case of brief quotations embodied in crit-
ical articles or reviews. For information, address St. Martin's Press,
175 Fifth Avenue, New York, N.Y. 10010.

Design by Judith Stagnitto.

Library of Congress Cataloging-in-Publication Data

Haywood. Gar.
    Fear of the dark / by Gar Anthony Haywood.
      p. cm.
    ISBN 0-312-01796-0
    I. Title.
PS3558.A885F4 1988   87-38237
813'.54—dc 19   CIP

First Edition
10 9 8 7 6 5 4 3 2 1

For My Father
JACK W. HAYWOOD

Whose wisdom I often mistook
for raving lunacy.

The white boy with the funny left eye walked into the Acey Deuce on a Monday Night Football night. It was odd timing for a man about to work this stranger's magic, as the club was usually packed on Mondays during the season and he was running the risk of being torn to pieces even before he could begin. But he was looking for headlines, trying to earn a certain reputation for reckless defiance, and mere survival had long ago been scratched from his list of personal priorities.

Ideally, in fact, he was hoping to play before a full house, one great writhing sea of black humanity that could stand witness to his power for years to come, but what he received for an audience instead was a handful of weary regulars who quite obviously had nowhere else to go. The Lions were hosting the Packers and combinations like that had a way of keeping people with any respect for the game away from giant-screen TVs.

September was in its waning days, but fall had not yet

turned up until tonight, however temporarily. If only to break the monotony of an unseasonal heat wave that was treating the good citizens of the city to a few more weeks of hell they didn't need, a cutting wind equal to anything Chicago had to offer forced its way through the rubble of what passed for a slum in south-central Los Angeles, bore down at the corner of 109th and Vermont, and nudged the white boy into the Deuce's stale warmth, wailing as it kicked the club's front door closed behind him.

While he waited for his pale, untenable eye to make friends with the darkness, standing motionless in the foyer like a cigar store Indian someone had kindly brought in from the cold, the Deuce's modest offering of black clientele and staff gazed in the stranger's direction and forgot their individual preoccupations. In the dim light of three wall-mounted beer signs and a few flickering candles, Buddy Dorris and Howard Gaines shoved aside a pile of dominoes at the bar; Mean Sheila and her latest meal ticket, a rail-thin youngblood from Detroit in town for a cousin's funeral, snuggled in a distant booth by the stereo and gave up trying to bring in a station they were too drunk to realize was broadcasting out of Irvine, almost sixty-five miles to the south; and J.T., the balding, bearded chunk of stout muscle who was both the club's owner and chief bartender, stood at a sink on the other side of the counter and poured a drink he had made for himself down the drain. J.T.'s wife Lilly was in attendance, as well, but the only indication of this was some muffled snoring the mistuned stereo was drowning out; she was asleep on a cot in the back storeroom, cases of Thunderbird surrounding her body like broken castle walls.

When he was comfortable in the Deuce's muted light, the white boy struck a pose for his hosts and grinned. This was not the crowd he had planned to entertain but the surprise, the uncertainty he had meant to arouse, was here, and it felt good to see it, to sense it, to taste it in the air. With open bravado he sauntered out of the shadows to the bar, grinding the ragged cuffs of his Levis together with each step, and claimed a seat only two stools down from Dorris, moving as if by rote. The temptation to laugh out loud was strong—the faces turned his way were too much—but he held his tongue and let the barflies squirm in an uncomfortable silence instead, knowing they would break it soon enough.

And of course, someone finally did, because a white man's intrusion into such segregated quarters as these was, on this night, at least, nothing if not a direct invitation to violence. Back in August, not so very long ago, this minor indiscretion, perhaps only an innocent mistake, could have easily been dismissed, forgiven like a child's first try at bold disobedience. But this was September, the dawn of a new and ugly season in the free world called America, and today leniency, for even the least of territorial crimes, was a difficult thing to come by, as the specter of a race war many thought inevitable was finally showing some teeth.

It was hoped by many that Black America was only making the noises of a people bracing for war—the disturbances that had so far broken out in New York, Miami, Houston, and some parts of the South had been riots in name alone—but given the respect the political machine presently in place in Washington seemed to have for its nonwhite constituency, maybe that was wishful thinking. The hand of ultraconservatism was turning back the clock on whatever progress American minorities had made in the last thirty years, striving to regain for those who held the power of the nation their long-lost freedom to close the doors of education and employment on whomever they damn well pleased, and it was becoming increasingly doubtful that this latest generation of black men and women with a good deal to lose was going to sit idly by and let it happen.

So if there had ever been a "good" time for a white man to crash the party at an all-black watering hole like the Acey Deuce (and there never had been, really) that time had most certainly passed, and no one had to draw J.T. a picture to make him see the jeopardy his beloved bar, and the livelihood that went with it, was suddenly in.

"What can I do for you?" the huge black man demanded of the white boy, in the voice his friends all knew meant his tolerance was on the wane.

He was edging his way over to the stranger's end of the bar as he spoke, making no pretense of stealth; there was a sawed-off ten-gauge mounted under the lip of the counter there, and that seemed like a smart place to be.

"You can help me find somebody," his new customer replied, and J.T. stopped moving, his worst suspicions confirmed all at once.

The white boy liked that—the bartender stopping on a dime, as if struck by something he hadn't seen coming—and smiled again to show his appreciation, not merely for J.T. but for the others as well. He seemed proud of his teeth but had no reason to be: his upper left incisor was missing and everything else was chipped and yellow, soon to follow.

Unlike the white boy, Buddy Dorris wasn't smiling. Once considered a misfit consumed by outdated politics, now looked upon as a sage for his dedication to those same, but newly fashionable, politics, he was a vocal advocate of revolutionary solutions to the oppression of his people, a hatemonger who worked diligently within the system to undermine it. He was only twenty-two, barely old enough to vote, but his rage was much older, a hand-me-down from generations past.

He turned to the white boy and asked, "Find who?"

And reciprocating, the white boy swiveled on his stool and said, "You."

His right hand was inside the shiny leather folds of his jacket before anyone could move, and out again by the time someone did. He caught Dorris lurching across the void between them and pointed the business end of an old Army Colt at the black man's face, pulling the trigger. The interior of the bar lit up with an angry red flare and Dorris's head became a spray of wet debris; his heavy frame caromed off Howard Gaines and fell to the floor, fragmented, lifeless. Gaines himself held his ground, reviewing the forty-three years of his life as a mop handle attachment in hurried flashbacks, but J.T. snatched the hidden shotgun free and managed to aim its muzzle in the white boy's general direction before the Army Colt spat twice more to drop him at the foot of the cash register, where his body lay under a rain of mixed liquor and splinters from the bar.

Mean Sheila was screaming like a banshee in the sudden descent of a relative silence. Gaines pressed his back against the wall behind him and tried to remember how to run, the acrid odor of wasted sulfur burning his nostrils, keeping him conscious. Out of the corner of his eye he could see Sheila's friend from Detroit cringing beneath the table of their booth, clinging to its one chrome leg the way a Kansas farmer, caught in the open, might have latched onto a tree to watch the black funnel of a tornado descend upon his homestead.

"Goddamn," he mumbled over and over, working to get the word out, whispering it at best. "Oh, *goddamn* . . ."

The white boy slipped down from his stool and began to take careful, backward steps toward the door. Mean Sheila stopped screaming to watch him hold his weapon high before him, swinging its flat nose from one remaining target to the next, lingering here, lingering there, making them guess his intentions. It was a game he was just beginning to enjoy when someone dropped something heavy in the back storeroom, beyond the door marked Employees Only. Sheila and Gaines knew it was only Lilly, coming around in her customary, graceless fashion, but the assassin did not, and now it was the others' turn to see fear in action. The white boy considered his options, his mad eye rolling in its socket like some runaway gyroscope, and hastily reverted to his retreat.

"The Brothers of Volition can go *fuck* themselves," he said when he reached the door, suddenly impassive, as if making but a casual observation. Shoving the pistol into the waistband of his pants he turned to run off, the beat of his boot heels on concrete fading slowly in his wake.

Not surprisingly, no one left alive at the Acey Deuce felt particularly inclined to follow.

It was an explosion that finally brought Aaron Gunner around.

An explosion or the doorbell, one or the other, the black man couldn't say for sure which. Perhaps it had been both.

He was recuperating from a losing bout with two bottles of Chivas Regal—not his brand of booze, why the hell had he bothered?—but Gunner found a working nerve ending and peeled one eye open. His bedroom window was open and a wave of glaring white sunlight, unimpeded by a pane of dusty glass, quickly rendered him blind.

He opened his other eye, blinking, and glanced at the digital clock on the nightstand beside his head. It was well past two in the afternoon. While he waited for more explosions he gave the day of the week some thought, decided it was Monday, reconsidered and settled for Tuesday, then rolled his 208 pounds out of bed, yawning.

He stood there in his bare feet, scratching himself, and

concluded that the doorbell was not going to ring again, if it ever had in the first place. He then limped to the bathroom and ran his hand over the barren landscape of his scalp, out of habit combing hair that had been gone for years. He thought of himself as an old man getting older, and to prove it he appraised himself in the mirror on the medicine cabinet door while urinating and suffered the usual disappointments. The tired lines beneath his sharp brown eyes were still there, and the stubble that grew over-night along the soft angles of his chin was getting harder to see every day—because it was white, as in gray, as in dying a slow death. Gunner was not an old man, but his was a face of charm worn down by thirty-four years of exhaustion, a handsome parchment of flesh he carried like a ledger filled with dreams that had died hard and hopes he had never coaxed off the ground. He smiled at it and watched a new wrinkle appear across his left cheekbone, yet another channel carved from his youth that he would have to learn to get used to.

He brushed his teeth at the sink, scrubbing the flavor of low-grade rocket fuel from the walls of his mouth, and headed for the kitchen, pausing to toss on a blue terry cloth robe that was draped over a chair in the hall. His home was like an oven but the robe was part of a ritual he couldn't find the energy to break; his elbow peeked out of a hole in the left sleeve.

The front of the little duplex was almost completely without light: all the shades were drawn, defending its inanimate tenants—a few pieces of fire-sale furniture and a refurbished hotel television—from the glare of the day outside. Dust particles danced silently in the rare strands of sunlight that broke through the cracks at windows and doors.

Gunner turned into the kitchen, yawning again, and reached for the handle of the refrigerator door. For once he didn't have to grope for it; it was caught in a band of bright light that shouldn't have been there, but the thought of a cold beer was fresh in his mind and the door was open in his hand before he could register the aberration.

"Don't move, Mr. Gunner," a cool voice warned him, lacking nothing in sincerity.

It was an order he had heard before, more than once. In the beginning, he liked to react to it according to his given mood, on some occasions following it to the letter, on others ignoring it altogether—but now he was older and wiser and less likely to survive internal hemorrhaging, and so he kept his hands where they were and closed his eyes, making no attempt to turn around. He knew without moving that he wouldn't recognize the lady that went with the voice, in any case.

"Are you alone?" he was asked.

"Yeah. You got a gun?"

"No girlfriends back there? A boyfriend, maybe?"

"No. I'm alone. Have you got a gun, or what?"

"What do you think?"

"I think you'd better have one. That's what I think."

He turned around. Old habits, like rituals, died hard.

His visitor started slightly. She was standing in the middle of the tile floor, thrusting the elongated snout of a revolver forward for his inspection. She was tall, but not too—five-eight, maybe five-ten—and black; her hips followed the telltale curve, and the fingers around the pistol's hilt were bronze, barely discernible from the dark metal of the weapon itself. He could see how she had come in: the door leading from his utility room was open behind her, giving him a clear view of his backyard lawn baking in the dry heat of yet another sweltering day.

"I told you not to move," she said, shaking.

He was trying to gauge her competency with firearms, but her stance was a mass of contradictions that made the task difficult, at best.

"There's thirty-three dollars and some change on a dresser in the bedroom, and a Timex watch on the coffee table in the living room. You might find a checkbook laying around somewhere, but the account's been closed for nine months."

"This isn't a rip-off," she said, by all indications insulted by the very idea. And yet she didn't go on to clarify exactly what it *was*.

"Jehovah's Witness?"

"No."

"Avon?"

"*Hell* no."

"Amway, the *Herald,* or *Encyclopedia Britannica*?"

She shook her head. "I'm not selling anything, Mr. Gunner. I'm buying."

"Buying? Buying what?" Gunner asked.

"Do you ever answer your phone? Or come to the door when people knock? I've been trying to reach you for *four days*. I've left notes in your mailbox, on your answering machine . . ."

"You were the one?"

"Too Sweet said you were good, that you knew your shit. He said you'd be a hard man to catch up with, but he didn't say you'd make it impossible."

"You've been talking to Too Sweet? Too Sweet Penny?"

The woman nodded.

"You're not looking for a private cop?"

She nodded again, gesturing with the gun, careful to remember why she was holding it. "Would I need *this* to hire an electrician?"

Gunner lowered his head and emptied his lungs with a weary, drawn-out sigh.

His friend didn't seem to notice. "I thought about coming without it," she said. "Taking this cat burglar approach to running you down seemed foolish enough as it was—but I'd heard some rather disturbing things about your temperament that led me to bring it along, just in case. I was afraid if I came empty-handed, you'd kill me before I could explain why I'd broken in this way."

"You mean there's a reason?"

"You didn't leave me much choice, did you? I've been trying to reach you for nearly a week, and for what? It was beginning to look like you might be dead, and I had to know if you were. Because I don't have another four days to waste, Mr. Gunner."

"Right. You're in a hurry."

"But obviously, you're okay."

"Obviously."

"And you're an experienced investigator, like Too Sweet says. You can walk on water, et cetera, et cetera."

"No. Could you put the gun down, Miss . . ?"

"No, what? No, you can't walk on water, or no, you're not experienced?"

"No, I'm not a cop. Experienced, or otherwise. The gun, sister, please."

"I don't understand."

"How about a cold beer? Or a cup of coffee?"

"You're telling me Too Sweet lied?"

"Can he do anything else? *Of course* he lied," Gunner said, exasperated. "Too Sweet's a boozer with good intentions but no common sense. He probably thought he was doing us both a favor, referring you to me, but he made a mistake. I'm out of the business. Have been for some time."

The girl held her ground, disoriented. "I don't believe you," she said firmly.

Gunner shrugged. "Apparently, neither does Too Sweet. But the fact remains, you're out of luck. Sorry."

He held his arms up in a gesture of regret, hoping some false sympathy would wash, but she pulled the hammer back on the gun with a long-nailed thumb, deliberately, making a sound that was impossible to misinterpret.

"You haven't heard me out, yet," she said.

Gunner watched her weapon float in an unsteady hand and said nothing. He still wasn't sure she knew how to use it but she was working from a range that made expertise pretty much irrelevant. If she could pull the trigger, she could get the job done, and if she had ever watched ten minutes of prime-time television, she could pull the trigger. In her sleep.

"All right," Gunner said, finally. "Say what you came to say and then get the hell out of here. I'm thirsty."

She paused, shifted on her feet, took a small step backward, and said, "I want you to find someone. A white man, with a bad left eye."

Gunner wasn't sure he had heard her right. "What?"

"He murdered my brother. Shot him in the face in a bar on 109th and Vermont, two weeks ago."

Gunner's eyes left the gun to meet hers. "The Acey Deuce."

"The Acey Deuce, right. He got the bartender there, too. A fat man named J.T. Tennell. You read about it, I guess."

The black man nodded, his mind wandering for a moment. It *was* a small world. Up until a year ago, the Deuce had been Gunner's primary hideout, and there was no reason to think his patronage would not have continued had his case load not begun the disappearing act that eventually prompted J.T. to pull the plug on his credit. To Lilly's great chagrin, J.T. had carried Gunner for four months, an astonishing length of time to be owed money for a bartender who, as his customers liked to say, poured a mean glass of water.

"Your brother was Dorris? Buddy Dorris?"

The girl nodded, bowing her head but once. "He was only twenty-two. Just a kid. Not much to brag about, maybe—he was shit to be around, really—but he didn't deserve to go like that. Splattered all over that wino's hole in the wall . . ."

She fell silent for a moment, resisting the urge to explode, then smiled a strange, jagged smile of remorse. "The mortician asked for three grand to put his head back together, but I didn't have it. So he put Buddy in the ground with a Baggie full of pieces tucked neatly under his pillow. Funny, huh?"

Gunner shuddered, involuntarily. He was gradually edging his body between the refrigerator and its open door, and the cold breath of the box was cutting through the pores of his robe to chill his back.

"That's rough," he said, meaning it.

"Yeah. Not a very popular guy, Buddy."

"The papers say the cops are looking for a Klansman."

The girl shrugged. "I guess that's a halfway logical place to start. Buddy *was* an outspoken individual. What you might call active in community affairs. That may have gotten him in trouble with some people, I suppose."

"'Some' people? Or just *white* people?"

"White people, primarily, sure. Hell, Buddy was a racist, why deny it? He started rallies and made big speeches long before that sort of behavior made its big comeback. Distributed pamphlets, the whole bit."

"For the Brothers of Volition."

"Yeah. That may not mean much today, but it would have eventually. Remember the Panthers? The Brothers were going to be bigger. Buddy was going to see to it."

Gunner didn't bother to refute that, just said, "Maybe they still will be. They've still got Roland Mayes."

"Roland Mayes, yeah." She laughed, seemingly more at Gunner than the thought. "He's the founder of the Brothers, and all that—their charismatic leader and focal point of what little press they get—but it was Buddy who made it all work, who supplied them with their drive and energy. I'd imagine that's why he was killed. The white boy probably understood—although Roland would never admit it—that Buddy's death will likely close the Brothers down sooner or later, and change the course of millions of lives in the process."

Gunner took a moment to bite his cynical tongue, then said, "That sounds like something a *Sister* of Volition might say."

She smiled. "It does, doesn't it? Must be indoctrination by osmosis. I've dropped in on the boys from time to time to hear what they have to say, of course, but that's as far as it goes. That political activism bit demands a certain level of commitment I haven't been able to attach to anything. So far."

Gunner turned a shoulder toward the gun in her hand and said, "You look pretty goddamned committed to me."

She shrugged again. "I need help. The police are working on Buddy's case the way you'd expect them to for a troublesome nigger. They're fucking around. So for some semblance of satisfaction, I thought I might turn to the private sector. Heroes for hire, mercenaries, whatever you want to call them. People like you. People with a price."

He watched her rub some imaginary bills between the thumb and forefinger of her free hand, the pistol listing slightly in the other, its muzzle never leaving the barrel of his chest for long. He was getting more acclimated to the kitchen's darkness, and the light pouring out of the refrigerator didn't hurt, but trying to make out the weapon's caliber was still about as easy as reading the sports page lining his garbage can several yards away. It was either a .22 or a long-nose .38, that much was safe to assume; she could graze his cheek with a slug from the latter and put him away with the concussion alone, but she'd have to find a major artery with the toy-like pellets of the former to do any real damage before he could reach out to wring her neck. Unless she went head-hunting at the last second . . .

Decisions, decisions.

"Look sister, I don't have a price for what you want. You could've rolled in here in a Brinks truck and I'd have had to tell you the same thing: I'm retired. Finished. No longer active in the investigative field."

"That's *bullshit*. You want to haggle about your fee, haggle. Whatever you think your time is worth, I'll pay. But don't try to tell me four days later I've come to see the wrong man."

14

"You want the Gospel truth? I couldn't find the guy who killed your brother if he were standing under a lampshade in my living room. Butt naked."

He was looking at the woman before him hard, only now seeing her clearly for the first time. She was smooth and brown, a living masterpiece of balanced angles and curves that stirred the wrong emotions in a man lately accustomed, and grimly resigned to, a celibate existence. Beauty was a relative commodity, a gift of the flesh often difficult to measure, but hers was the kind you could see just fine in the dark, at close or distant quarters.

. "I mean, for Chrissake, look around! Does this look like the home of a *winner* to you?"

He poked his jaw at the shambles of his estate, trying to take his mind off the erection growing rapidly beneath his robe.

The girl with the gun put her teeth on display in a slanted grin and laughed again. "It looks like the home of a man who could use the gig," she said.

Gunner's left hand dove over the refrigerator door and grabbed her right wrist, pinching the nerves there in a vise.

The gun went off once, harmlessly; the .22-caliber bullet hit the thick wall of the old refrigerator's door at an awkward angle and bounced off in the direction of some grease stains on the wall above the stove. Staying behind the door in relative safety, Gunner threw a straight right hand at the girl's jaw and didn't miss. Her gun reached the linoleum floor before she did, but it was a close race down.

Gunner took possession of the revolver, dropped its shells into the pocket of his robe, and watched the woman at his feet sleep. He had been afraid that, once the time came to make his move, he would instinctively pull his punch, succumbing to his incurable flair for chivalry despite the lady's hostile posture, but her crack about his living quarters had made throwing a loaded right hand something to look forward to. He wasn't coping with the quality of his life very well these days.

Pulling a beer out of the refrigerator at last, he kicked a kitchen chair to the center of the room and sat down to wait for the late Buddy Dorris's pushy sister to come around. What he should have done was dump her body at the curb out front, to make a point and reach a quick decision, but he let her stretch out on his kitchen floor instead, and took the next few minutes to reconsider his retirement, to question his judgment, just one more time.

Introspection, as always, was a walk down the road to nowhere.

The problem was, he was lousy.

He had been lousy at the beginning, and was lousy in the end. He gave private investigation everything he had, but it had always been, and always would be, a compromise profession.

When the LAPD booted him out of its cadet academy for rearranging the face of an overzealous self-defense instructor in October of 1974, going into private practice seemed like the only logical alternative. It lacked the glamour and drama of legitimate police work, but a badge and an ironclad gun permit came with the territory and that made it the next best thing.

Why he cared to be involved in law enforcement at all was a mystery he could explain to no one's satisfaction. He had no hang-up regarding power of the life-and-death variety; by the first month of a year-long stint in Vietnam almost seventeen years ago, he had killed enough people in the interests of "duty" to grow tired of the thrill forever. And as for the law itself, he was less than enamored by its credibility. Crime and punishment was a fine concept, perhaps, but in the real world he had never seen it work indiscriminately, which was to say he had never seen it work at all.

But something about wearing a badge and attaching himself to the things it represented seemed ideal, once his days in the service had come to an end, and only after months of living with it was he able to recognize the attraction for what it was: a need to *belong*. Freshly removed from the cut-and-dried order of war, where everything functioned in a beautifully simplistic either/or system, black or white, Us or Them, he was desperate to align himself with a cause and its following, preferably one diametrically opposed to another. His hunger was not for camaraderie, but for a sense of identity, some specific role to play in the free-for-all chaos that was civilian life.

It would have been convenient to have more than one bipartisan conflict suited to his needs to choose from, but Gunner wasn't that lucky. He was living in an age in which conviction to causes was out of vogue and apathy was often confused with open-mindedness. If people took up sides at all, they didn't talk about it, an abstention that left the world virtually impossible to dissect into finite philosophical factions. The only line drawn between men that remained indelible was the law. Corruption was blurring that line more every day—money *did* talk, and everyone, it so often appeared, was listening—but the illusion of just men waging war against the forces of darkness was still intact in the realm of law enforcement, and for Gunner the lost lamb, an illusion seemed good enough.

He took his rude rejection by the LAPD badly, but moved quickly on to a junior college education spread out over two short years and four different schools that eventually earned him a private investigator's license, a cheap piece of paper that entitled him to play a few grown-up games with the state of California's blessings. He set to work enthusiastically, as motivated as he could hope to be toward a trade that only emulated the real thing, but it was a lost cause almost immediately. He had no feel for the work, no natural aptitude for its nuances. His delusions of self-worth and identification with something tangible were short-lived.

He didn't have to spend many nights in motel parking lots, waiting for one client or another's stray spouse to cut an incriminating pose for his Polaroid, to understand what he had become and where he was headed: nothing and nowhere, respectively. His authority had no teeth; he could quote the law but not defend it. He was just a man with a dime store ID card in his wallet, a cardboard "pig" you could use for a target range without fear of repercussions, a Peeping Tom who had the right to ask questions no one had to answer. Even when business was good, and it was never good for long, it was bad; his successes were devoid of accomplishment and his failures only confirmed his growing sense of impotence. Efficiency was hard to come by on the heels of perpetual insecurity.

And yet it had taken Al Dobey to make Gunner quit.

Dobey had shown up at Gunner's door at a bad time, the height of a famine that had seen the detective pour his meals from a cornflakes box for nineteen days and nights. Dobey was a pimp with a weight problem, a coke-head and compulsive liar. But any man with a proposition was someone Gunner had to hear out, like it or not, and Dobey seemed genuinely desperate to pay for the investigator's services. He had a fourteen-year-old daughter who had taken off without warning, left for school one day and never come back, and he wanted Gunner to find her. She was his only link to decency, he said, and to illustrate his fatherly grief, he dried his eyes with the palms of his hands like an old woman at a funeral.

It was a performance Gunner didn't buy for one minute, knowing Dobey's well-earned reputation as a prince among scumbags, but he thought about his last bowl of cornflakes and took the pimp's retainer anyway.

Audra Dobey was supposed to be a wild and rebellious kid, too much like her father for her own good, but when Gunner turned her up six days later, he couldn't see the family resemblance. She was a cute, frail little thing hiding out in a duplex on Wilton near Slauson with a girlfriend and the girl's older brother. If she needed a good reason for running away, she had the best: she was four months pregnant and showing from every angle. It would have been smart to ask her how she got that way, but Gunner was feeling more hungry than smart at the time; he kept out of sight and tipped Dobey to her whereabouts by phone.

Two weeks later he was back on the streets all over again, this time looking for Dobey and his fee. The pimp's was suddenly a cold trail, save for a single newsflash that eventually made the rounds to the angry black man he had left behind like a bloodhound off the scent: Audra was dead. Her father had forced her into a discount abortion and somebody's hand had slipped. There were cops combing the neighborhood in Gunner's wake suggesting she had been carrying Dobey's child. It wasn't such a far-fetched idea.

Gunner managed to live with the guilt for four days. Parked across the street in the wee hours of a Thursday morning, he was watching the assistant manager of an ABC market on Vernon and Vermont load a few frozen turkeys into the trunk of his car when the futility of Gunner's existence finally touched the wrong nerve and the detective knew he had had enough.

In eleven years he had learned to wade through the pus of humanity for money, to pocket a few dollars and scrape the earth for garbage his clients weren't willing to touch, but he had never once done it for free. He let the turkey thief go about his business and drove home, where he finished off the last remnant of Dobey's forty-five-dollar retainer—a fifth of Wild Turkey—in record time.

He had been an electrician ever since.

His cousin Del had been offering to take him on as an apprentice for years and had welcomed Gunner aboard with open arms. There wasn't much excitement in running wire through a maze of conduits, twisting one's body to fit into cramped crawlspaces where mice often kept you company, but regular meals were part of the deal and the work took no toll on the human spirit. Gunner's days of waiting for something to happen were over. The false expectations and unrealized drama of private investigating were behind him, and the lies of time-honored pulp novels were now for other fools to believe.

So the lady on the floor of his kitchen was flat out of luck. No matter what his friends had told her—they just couldn't see him as an electrician for long—he was through beating holes in his shoes playing shadow to unfaithful wives and larcenous employees, runaway adolescents and killers of left-wing militants, and he wasn't going back for anybody or anything. It made no difference what she did to his libido, what she was willing to spend, or how far she was prepared to go to hire him. He wasn't interested. He wasn't tempted.

Much.

Signs of life—a shifting of the left arm, the rearrangement of feet—began to appear before Gunner's eyes.

The beauty on his kitchen floor, the sister the press apparently didn't know Buddy Dorris had, came around at last and sat up, testing the joint of her jaw for function. Gunner gulped down the last of his third beer and tossed the empty can across the room to get her attention.

"You got a name?" he asked.

"Fuck you," she said.

"Hurts pretty bad, huh?"

"If you broke it, I'll kill you. I swear it." She started looking around on the floor for her gun.

"It's over here," Gunner said.

He let her see the .22, the same end she'd offered him to view only minutes ago. Its threat was clearer since he'd parted the curtains on the little kitchen window, but she didn't seem to mind.

"You made your point, all right? You don't need my business."

"Maybe it wasn't your business I objected to. Maybe it was the fucked-up way you went about presenting it."

Silence.

"You got a name?" he asked again.

Her hands fell away from her jaw, slowly. "Verna."

"Verna what?"

"Verna Gail. G-A-I-L, Gail. Are you going to help me, or what?"

"That your married name, 'Gail'?"

"Yes."

"Where is Mister Gail right now?"

"Safe from the demands of alimony. Meaning he's dead. You didn't answer my question, Mr. Gunner."

Gunner made her wait a long time for an answer; she had done all the interrogating she was going to do in his house. "I don't remember ever hearing that Buddy Dorris *had* a sister," he said.

"Who have you been talking to?"

"No one, yet. But it bears looking into, don't you think? I mean, one wouldn't necessarily have to be related to Buddy Dorris to want a piece of the man who killed him. Would one?"

"I told you. Buddy was my brother. *Biologically.* Would you take my case if I could prove that?"

"I don't know. Possibly. I haven't heard what happens to the white man once I find him, yet. You haven't gone to all this trouble just to get him off the street."

"No." Her eyes were suddenly cold, fixed on a target only she could see. "I haven't."

"You intend to kill him, or just bust him up real good?"

"I don't know. I haven't made up my mind, yet."

"You have somebody lined up to take care of that end? Or were you counting on me to do it?"

"Would you?"

"Hell, I don't see why not. Accessory to murder, murder, it's all the same thing to the D.A. What's another life sentence tacked on to the first?"

He laughed at her blank reaction to that, the mute surprise of a spiteful little girl with a serpent's eyes and an angel's face. He watched her bite her lower lip, waiting for him to go on, until it became apparent that he wasn't going to oblige.

"You think I should just let the police have him. Is that it?"

Gunner didn't say anything.

"They'd only try him and let him go. You know that."

"Maybe. Maybe not. But I'll tell you what I do know: I'm getting tired of this asinine negotiating. So I'm going to make it as simple for you as I can: *I won't set him up for you.* He either belongs to the Man once I find him, or you can find him yourself. Or grab a copy of the Yellow Pages and start looking for someone else who will."

His eyes were fixed upon her, but following his gaze, she realized it was not deliberate: she had opened her blouse generously in her sleep, and the soft arc of ample cleavage was exposed to the open air. She watched him avert his eyes as she made repairs and said, "You act as if I need you more than you need me."

Gunner grinned, trying to hide his embarrassment. "Don't you? Or has some other soul brother opened up shop in the neighborhood I don't know about?" He laughed again, painfully. "Worries I've got, sister, but competition's not one of 'em. I've seen the phone book, I know."

"So you've got the market all to yourself," she said. "So what? Supply reflects demand. If you're the only P.I. on the black-hand side of the world, it's probably only because there's not enough work out here for two. I'll bet mine's the first offer you've had in *months.*"

"That doesn't mean I have to take it."

She glowered at him coldly, her body completely motionless. "You've got as much choice as I do."

Gunner didn't argue.

"I want the man who killed my brother, Mr. Gunner. And you want me. Isn't that right?"

She was staring at the mound a new erection was forming with the folds of his robe. He hadn't been with a woman in her class for a long time, and the memory of what it had been like wouldn't go away.

"I won't set him up for you," he told her again, swallowing hard.

She smiled, assuming all the control he could sense himself relinquishing. "All right. Turn him in, if you want. It won't change anything." She laughed. "I'll get my crack at him, sooner or later. At the trial, maybe."

"If I can find him."

"You'll find him. You're supposed to be cheap. Not incompetent."

She laughed again, resting her head on one shoulder, as Gunner watched her in restless silence, fully regretting what he was about to do.

"You get what you pay for, Verna Gail," he said dryly, flipping her empty gun through the air toward her. "Remember that."

She caught the gun awkwardly, sensing his abrupt change of mood, and through doleful eyes watched as he came up slowly from his chair to approach her, allowing his robe to open as it pleased.

2

Gunner said, "I won't be coming in today, Del," and left it at that. His cousin would know what to make of the silence that followed, even over the phone.

"Don't tell me," Del said.

"Something came up. A one-shot deal. Ought to take me a week to handle at the most."

"Uh-huh. A one-shot deal." He instigated a silence of his own. "You can lead a horse to water, but you can't make him drink. Ever hear that?"

"A few days, Del. I'll be back to work in a few days."

"I'll hold my breath," Del said, and hung up.

It was two o'clock in the afternoon at the Acey Deuce, and Gunner couldn't find a seat at the bar. He hadn't been around to look for one in over a year, but his recollection of Wednesdays at the Deuce was clear, and they had been nothing like this, at any time of the day.

Bobbing in and out of an expansive storm cloud of cigarette smoke that lent total obscurity to the far reaches of the room, black people milled about the establishment in varied states of inebriation, controlling every seat in the house save for one booth by the door, where a table leg reached up from the floor into thin air, in search of a missing tabletop. The dress code was liberal, a perfect indicator of the oppressive heat on the street; homemade cut-offs and K-Mart tanktops were the order of the day. It was a lively group, boisterous and uninhibited, but laughter was in short supply, a curiosity Gunner was quick to notice.

He peered over the rolling wave of heads lining the bar, offering himself up to the welcome embrace of the Deuce's air conditioning, and spotted Lilly pouring a drink on the other side of the counter. She was bigger than he remembered her; the apron around her waist looked like a bed sheet and her throat was one great balloon of fat, a cushion upon which to rest her massive head. Her face was the kind a smart woman drew as little attention to as possible, but she still hadn't figured that out: her trademark smear of blood-red lipstick made her lips stand out in the darkness like a flare marking the night.

Gunner was hoping her heart had grown in direct proportion to her girth since they last had met, but he knew that wasn't likely. Lilly's good nature had never been the most fully developed aspect of her character, and J.T.'s violent death could not have done much to improve it. Unless her late husband—love struck fool that he was—had left her more in the way of an estate than the Acey Deuce represented, the odds were good she would greet Gunner's return to the premises with all the warmth of a cold fried egg.

Finding a tiny gap between two occupied stools at the bar and wedging his body into it, Gunner leaned on the counter with his left elbow and waited to catch Lilly's eye. She kept him waiting, perhaps deliberately, perhaps not, moving to the far end of the bar to serve another customer and add some color to an otherwise dying argument being waged there. He watched her for a while and then surveyed the place, looking for a familiar face, but the only one that rang any bells belonged to Howard Gaines, who was sharing a bowl of mixed nuts with two young men at a table in the center of the room. They were washing the nuts down with beer—Colt 45 in bottles—and were using their hands extensively while they talked.

When Gunner again turned his head to find Lilly he was nearly perversely kissed: she was standing directly in front of him, bracing herself against the bar with both hands like a Bekins man moving a piano.

"What do you want, nigger?" she asked matter-of-factly, as soft and personable as ever.

"Lilly," Gunner grinned, liking her style. "What's happening?"

"What's happenin' is news. News is in the newspaper. This is a bar. You want somethin' to drink?"

"That would be nice."

"Let me see a U.S. president." She held her hand out, palm up, and waited. "Jackson, Lincoln, Hamilton—anybody but Washington. Only thing Washington's good for in here is change for the phone."

Gunner pulled a hundred-dollar bill from his trouser pocket and displayed its face for her inspection. "How about Ben Franklin? He was never president, but he flew a mean kite."

Lilly frowned at the bill and put a clean shot glass on the bar in front of him. "Turkey and water, I suppose?"

Gunner's head rocked up and down affirmatively. She was murder on names, but the woman could remember a man's drink like it was written on his forehead, even when it was dependent upon the nature of his luck at the moment. Most people drank the same thing religiously, rain or shine, but Lilly, like J.T. before her, had long ago learned that Gunner preferred name-brand rotgut—Ten High, Kessler, Lord Calvert—when the rattle of loose change followed his every step, and Wild Turkey, and Wild Turkey alone, on the rare occasions when bills of high denomination came with his usual dose of jive.

"Sorry to hear about J.T.," he said as she worked on his drink, meaning it more than his voice had conveyed.

The big woman looked him straight in the eye and said, "Bullshit. He called in your marker and you ain't been back since. Now he's dead, you wanna drop in to run up a new tab. Now tell me that ain't right."

"It ain't right."

"Bullshit."

Four stools down to Gunner's right, a short man in a greasy Midas Muffler uniform was calling Lilly's name for the third time, waving an empty beer bottle over his head like a pennant at a football game, but the Deuce's new owner wouldn't dignify his efforts with so much as a glance. She was looking forward to telling Gunner off, and putting pleasure before business had always been her modus operandi.

"You're a poor judge of character, Lilly," Gunner told her, shaking his head before sampling the firewater in his glass. He held the warm liquid in his mouth for a long beat, then passed it down his throat slowly, patiently, relishing the experience. It was beginning to look like a good week for renewing old friendships with life's simple pleasures.

"Uh-huh. I got you all wrong, Gunner. It's just coincidence, you showin' up today. Now that the man of the house ain't around to kick your lyin' ass out."

"As a matter of fact, it's not a coincidence, exactly. If J.T. were still alive, I probably wouldn't be here."

"Tell me about it."

"Okay, Lilly. Enough with the amenities. Buddy Dorris's big sister's hired me to find the guy who killed Buddy and J.T. The white man with the dynamite baby blues. Now you'd like to see me pull that off, wouldn't you?"

She chuckled at the thought. "I ain't gonna live that long," she said.

"Okay, so the lady's reckless with her bread. I tried to

tell her that myself, but she wouldn't take no for an answer. She seems to like my chances of finding the guy, at least better than the Man's. Slim is better than none, right?"

Lilly remained silent. The thirsty Midas employee down the bar was getting belligerent.

"Or do you think the cops are busting their behinds on the case?"

"Hmph. They ain't doin' jack shit."

"There you go." Gunner picked up his glass and stood up, nodding his head toward the open booth with the missing counter top. "Come on over here and talk to me for a minute. Just to answer a few questions. Take a break."

She didn't move right away. A break sounded good to her but she wasn't at all sure Gunner could make reliving her husband's death for the ten-thousandth time worthwhile.

"Lilly," Gunner prodded. "The boy will be a million miles gone if somebody doesn't start looking for him soon. Either you give me a hand or he'll walk, free and clear. That what you want?"

It was a supposition he only half-believed himself, but he knew it was the last thing Lilly wanted to hear. She seemed on the brink of making a decision when her friend in the unkempt Midas uniform finally managed to get her attention. Stretched out diagonally across the bar, his diminutive legs flailing about, unhindered by the floor, he was trying to pull a fresh Budweiser from the open ice bay behind the counter, making quite a mess. An amused audience was cheering him on, hoping he would lose his balance and fall. They got their wish, but only because Lilly rushed over to protect her merchandise and shoved him with both hands back out of her territory, cursing expansively. A valid swell of laughter erupted throughout the club for the first time since Gunner's arrival, and it was a welcome if momentary return to the Deuce of old.

When Lilly had made peace with all the neglected

souls at the bar, she waddled around it to join Gunner again, untying her apron strings as she walked.

"Bar's closed!" she shouted, throwing the apron over her shoulder stylishly. "I'm takin' twenty minutes!"

There was a light rumble of dissent, but she ignored it. "Let's talk," she said to Gunner, and headed for the crippled booth by the door.

"I was asleep in the back when it happened. Never did see the sonofabitch."

"Yeah?"

"The newspapers left that out, didn't they? Everybody thinks I saw the whole thing, but I missed it completely. By the time I came around and ran up front, the white boy was out the door, and J. and Buddy were dead."

She was sucking on a narrow, dark-skinned Sherman cigarette for all it was worth, keeping her eyes on the cash register all the while.

"I never seen so much blood in all my life. On the floor, the stools. I had to have a guy come in to replace the tiles behind the bar and a whole section of wall panelin' at the end there. You can see the difference if you look hard enough." She pointed to a spot on the far wall where the plastic woodgrain's fraudulence was more distinguishable than at any other point in the room. "That's where Buddy got it. J. was over by the sink. He'd made it to the piece we keep under the bar, but they say he never got off a shot. That man was slow, Lord knows."

Gunner watched her eyes lose their focus and asked who besides Buddy had been there that night. He had to keep things moving at a fast clip if he wanted to hold her attention and keep depression at bay.

She blew more smoke into the air and said, "Just Howard and Sheila, that's all. Our air conditionin' was out that week and business had been lousy for days. Turned out it was cold as hell that night, but that afternoon had been a bitch like all the others, and I guess nobody had the strength to drop by. I would've stayed away myself, if J. hadn't made me come in to take inventory."

"Sheila was alone?"

"Oh, I forgot. She had some sweetpea from back East with her. A cousin from Detroit, or somethin' like that. He was a sissy, a stone sissy. Hid under a table at one of the booths and wouldn't come out. The police talked to him for fifteen minutes, but he just stayed down there, cryin'. I told Sheila if she didn't get him out from under there, I was gonna do it myself. I guess he heard me."

"He still in town?"

"I don't think so. Ask Sheila."

"You get his name?"

Lilly shrugged. "Ray or Roy, somethin' like that. I was in the back when they came in, so we were never properly introduced."

Gunner looked out over the crowd again, absently playing with the ice cubes in his otherwise empty glass. The bartender's respite had sent a few customers packing, but breathing space at the Deuce was still conspicuously missing.

"I don't see Sheila around today," Gunner said.

Lilly shook her head. "She hasn't been in for weeks. It really shook her up, seein' J. and Buddy get killed like that. She don't go out much of anywhere anymore, from what I hear. But Howard's around. See him over there at that middle table? Sittin' with Frank and Ricky Lott?"

She waved her apron in Gaines's direction, but Gunner didn't bother to look. "I saw him when I came in," he said.

"You gonna talk to him?"

"That would seem the logical thing to do."

"Want me to go get him?"

"If you feel up to it, yeah. I don't know the Lotts and they don't know me, and the fewer people who know I'm working on this, the better."

Lilly nodded and pushed herself up from the booth,

looking like a dirigible low on helium fighting for lift-off. She forced her way through a crush of bodies to Gaines's table and whispered something in his ear, smiling. He looked up to spot Gunner across the room and his head bobbed up and down in a generous nod. He bid the Lott brothers a quick but congenial farewell and stood up, then followed the path Lilly made for him over to Gunner's booth.

"Hey, Gunner. Where you been keepin' yourself, man?"

Gaines smothered the investigator's fist in both hands, lovingly, up among the clouds after a six-pack lunch. He was one of Gunner's favorite people, despite the annoying fact that getting tipsy only made him more gushingly affectionate than he was ordinarily.

"Lilly tells me you're workin' for Buddy's sister," he said, sitting down beside the bartender.

Gunner nodded. "You know her?"

"I met her once or twice. At them rallies Buddy was always talkin' me into goin' to. Her name's Verna, right?"

"Verna Gail, yeah."

"Yeah, Verna Gail. She's got you lookin' for the fool that killed Buddy and J.T.?"

Gunner nodded again.

"Man, good luck. As hot as we've made it for white folks around here, that boy might never show his face in daylight again. Not here, not anywhere."

Suddenly, the bar's dark mood made sense. "Is that what all these people are doing? Waiting for him to come back?"

"It's as good a place to look for him as any."

"Shit," Lilly said gruffly, "that man ain't comin' back here. He got what he came for the last time." She grinned. "But don't expect me to tell no payin' customer that."

Her grin broke into laughter, as she bubbled with admiration for her own keen business sense.

"You mean Buddy," Gunner said.

Gaines nodded feverishly, but Lilly snapped, "No! That ain't what I mean! That's what everybody thinks, but that's a lie."

"Shit," Gaines said.

"I don't care what anybody says. It was J. that white boy was after, I know it."

"You weren't even in here," Gaines argued, turning a narrowed eye upon her. "How the hell would you know?"

He looked at Gunner and said, "The man came in and said he was lookin' for somebody. Just like that, bold as you please, a white man lookin' for somebody at the Deuce, with people as hot and things as crazy as they been right now. Buddy asked him who he was lookin' for, and the white man said, 'You.' Next thing you know, he's got a gun in his hand, and Buddy's the first to get it. If J.T. hadn't grabbed that piece from under the bar, he might never've got shot at all."

"Bullshit," Lilly said.

"He never asked for money or nothin'," Gaines continued, letting her comment pass. "The cops wanted me to say it was robbery, but it wasn't. I told 'em, shit, I seen a robbery once, I know how they go down. This was murder, man, all the way."

"And Buddy was his man."

"Absolutely."

"Bullshit," Lilly said again.

Gunner turned to her. "Lilly. Baby. Who in the world would want to kill J.T.?"

"You don't wanna hear this," Gaines moaned.

Gunner waved him off and Lilly said, "Sweet Lou."

Which, true to Gaines's word, was something Gunner didn't care to hear.

What interest could a drug-runner in entrepreneur's clothing like "Sweet" Lou Jenkins have in the death of a barkeeper on the opposite side of town?

"Sweet Lou?"

Lilly nodded. He had been afraid she would.

"I didn't think they knew each other," he said.

"They didn't. J. wouldn't have nothin' to do with Lou, everybody knows that."

"So why should Lou want to kill him?"

Lilly lifted her huge shoulders up in a ponderous shrug, then let them drop. "I don't know," she said. "All I know is J. got a call from that college boy pimp who works for Lou a few days before he died. You know the one I mean?"

"Price," Gaines said, if only to speed things along.

"Price, right. The fashion plate lawyer with the fancy mouth and pretty car. He called J. here at the club and got him all hot and heavy, had him talkin' about killin' people, and shit. J. took the call back in the office, and closed the door so I wouldn't hear what he was sayin', but he raised enough hell that I got the gist of it anyway, even out here workin' the bar. It had somethin' to do with Lou wanting a piece of the Deuce, I think. J. must've said, 'Stay the fuck away from my place' about fifty times before he hung up."

"You ask him about it afterward?" Gunner asked.

"Of course. And I still got the marks to prove it."

"He wouldn't talk about it."

"No. He said it was just Deuce business, nothin' for me to worry about. He was gonna handle it, he said."

"You ever actually hear him mention Sweet Lou by name?"

"No."

"Or Price?"

"No. But I was the one answered the phone. The boy says, 'Let me speak to J.T.,' right to the point, no hello or nothin'. I asked him, 'Who should I say is callin'?' and he just says, 'Tell him it's in regards to our recent dialogue at the Kitchen.' Now how many niggers *you* know use the word 'dialogue' like that?"

It was Gunner's turn to shrug. "A few. You read something other than *Jet* once a month, that'll happen to you."

"Not to nobody callin' here, it don't."

"Okay. So it was Lou's man Price on the phone. Go on."

The big woman stared at him. "Go on, what?"

Gunner stared back. "So where does Sweet Lou come in?"

"He don't," Gaines said, shaking his head skeptically.

Lilly glared at him and said, "Who owns the Kitchen, Howard? And who else around here works hand-in-hand with white people every day?"

"Lilly, I keep tellin' you, the boy that shot J.T. and Buddy didn't work for Sweet Lou! He was poor white trash, probably a bigger 'literate than anybody you know, and that ain't Sweet Lou's speed. Lou uses class people, white, black, and otherwise, and nothin' else but. Ain't that right, Gunner?"

"So they say."

"He *could've* worked for Sweet Lou," Lilly insisted stubbornly.

"Not the man *I* saw," Gaines argued, his patience wearing thin. "The man I saw, Lou wouldn't've hired to change a flat."

"Describe the guy," Gunner said, pulling a small notebook from his shirt pocket. He borrowed a pen from Lilly and turned to one side to use the backrest of the booth for support as he took notes. Gaines painted a surprisingly complete portrait of someone he had seen only once for a man whose own vocabulary was nothing to brag about.

"You ever see him before?" Gunner asked, almost rhetorically. "Or since?"

"No," Gaines said, "but . . ." He had a pained expression on his face.

"But what?"

"This ain't gonna help you any, 'cause it don't exactly come from a reliable source. But Sheila said she had. Seen him before, that is." His eyes were on Lilly, expecting the news to get a rise out of her.

Lilly only laughed.

"Like I said. It don't come from a reliable source," Gaines said.

Gunner wasn't laughing. "She say *where* she thought she'd seen him before?"

Gaines shook his head. "Not to me. And I heard what she told the cops that night, and she didn't tell them shit. She played dumb and went home soon as they let us all go. I seen her a few days after that, in Ralph's market, and that's when she told me. She was all messed up about it, scared to be seen anywhere. She figured the boy had recognized her, too, and was lookin' to shut her up. You should've seen her rushin' to get in and out of that market."

"Have you spoken to her since?"

"No."

"Who else knows about this? Anybody?"

"Nobody. Who'm I gonna tell that believes anything Sheila's got to say? I don't believe it myself."

"You don't."

"No. But I believe *she* believes it. Ain't that what those shrinks on TV always say?"

Gunner looked at Lilly. She said, "Hey, I told you, she ain't been in here. And if she had, she'd have known better than to tell *me* she'd seen that funny-eyed mother-fucker before. I'd have found out where, or killed her tryin'."

Gunner asked Gaines if he knew the full name of Sheila's partner the night of J.T. and Buddy's murder.

"Ray Hollins," Gaines said. "Said he was a fighter out of Detroit, Golden Glove just turned pro in the feather-weight division, but he didn't look like no fighter to me." He winked at Lilly and the two of them had a good laugh.

Gunner asked what Hollins did look like, and Gaines told him, sketching yet another vivid picture of a perfect stranger.

"Sheila likes those skinny ones, I think," he said, chuckling.

Gunner was putting his notebook away. He put Lilly's pen in his pocket, too, and got away with it.

Gaines asked, "You gonna go see her, huh?"

Gunner nodded. "Why not?"

"Hey, if you got to, you got to. Maybe she's tellin' the truth for once in her life, who knows? But I tell you what—you go over there, you better step light." He took the detective's hand again and said, "'Cause that girl was crazy to begin with. Now she's all wound up, she could be dangerous. *Downright* dangerous."

"I hear you, Howard," Gunner said.

"Besides, you know what she always says: 'Just 'cause I'm paranoid . . .'"

"'. . . that don't mean they ain't out to get me.' Yeah, I remember."

Gunner made it to his feet and winked at his friends, grinning.

"I say it all the time myself," he said, and walked out before it could dawn on Lilly that he was starting up a new tab, after all.

3

The name on her California driver's license—which had expired more than two years ago—was Sheila Denise Pulliam, but everybody called her Mean Sheila. Those who were unaware of the story behind the nickname could not understand how she could have possibly earned it, for in truth she was a pussycat, warm and outgoing and generous to a fault. They didn't know about the four-year stretch she had pulled at the Georgia Rehabilitation Center for Women in the late seventies, or the boyfriend-turned-pimp she had murdered to get there.

Back in the late spring of '83, Sheila had come west following her early release from prison with the vague hope that she could make the kind of money on her back in Los Angeles no whore could aspire to in Athens, Georgia. She fully expected something less than the paradise propaganda consistently promised, but the overcrowded world of has-beens and losers she came to find dealt her a devastating blow nevertheless. The City of Angels's reputation as the motherlode of opportunity turned out to be one it deserved, to her mild surprise, but her advisers in Georgia had failed to acquaint her with a fact simple mathematics could have easily pointed out: where opportunity knocks, desperate people rush *en masse* to answer its call. Hookers like Sheila, pouring forth in daily waves from the terminals at LAX and boarding platforms at Grand Central Station, were as rare in California as a good tan, and just as valuable.

And there was only so much Solid Gold to go around.

So Sheila had settled into impoverished mediocrity without a great deal of struggle and made L.A. her home. At thirty-three she was too tired to do anything else. She worked the Inglewood district for two years under the guidance of a rookie flesh peddler named Pee Wee, then went independent and moved her wares thirteen miles south to Compton, where she enjoyed a fair amount of prosperity. Independence would have cost most working girls some teeth, but Sheila wasn't the youngest piece in Pee Wee's stable and he was constantly having to apologize for her refusal to perform a good third of the day's most popular acts of perversion. He let her go almost gladly. She played around in Hollywood for a while, but the fierce competition and high risk of arrest drove her back to the inner city. She bought a tiny house that sat behind a larger one on the 2200 block of 153rd and let a trickle of steady neighborhood business supplement the wages of welfare.

Gunner had known Sheila for well over two years, but had never made the trip to her place of residence until now. She was hot for his body, always had been, and he disliked his chances of fending her off on her own turf, convinced as he was that any sexual contact between them would do irreparable harm to both their friendship and his appreciation of sex with living partners.

On this day, however, standing on the balding patch of lawn that served as both the backyard of the large home facing the street and the front yard of Sheila's smaller unit to the rear, Gunner assumed that seduction would be the last thing on Sheila's mind. Howard Gaines and Lilly had described her as a petrified recluse, a woman of already questionable courage afraid for her life, and if he was at all uneasy about being here—and there was no point in denying that he was—it was strictly due to his ignorance of the devices she had on hand to protect herself with. Devices he had no doubt the slightest provocation would lead her to use, no questions asked.

Gingerly, then, he checked the windows of the tiny four-room cottage she lived in for indications of life, but the curtains were drawn and too thick with dust to see through. Rather than press his nose to the glass to get a better look—the blazing afternoon sun would make him all too easy to see from inside as it was—he moved on to the door of the little house and rang a bell that didn't appear to be working. He left the bell alone and started to knock politely on the door. A dog somewhere behind him used the racket as an excuse to make some noise of its own, and he turned around to watch a good-sized Doberman claw at the screen door of the main house's back porch, acting like an animal that hadn't seen red meat in months.

Made to feel like an open-face sandwich, Gunner sped his business along and tried the door, which he expected to find locked. Leaning slightly forward to set his weight against it, he sprawled unceremoniously into the dark house when someone inside jerked the door wide open and stepped aside, into the shadows.

Gunner caught his balance before hitting the floor and ducked a poor right hand his unseen host threw at the back of his head, but took a left hook with better aim flush on the chin. He staggered backward, farther into the blackness of the room, and a straight right tried to follow the left, but this one he sensed coming and let go by, countering with two sharp rights of his own, throwing them where he judged a kidney to be and hitting pay dirt. What felt like a lightweight body doubled up around his hand, and the narrow face of a young black man with the ghost of a mustache dropped clearly into view, bathed in a tight wedge of sunlight the open front door was welcoming into the house.

Gunner launched a hard left at the nose above the mustache and the sound of bone meeting bone rang sharply through the air. The stranger took a short flight back into obscurity and came to rest Gunner knew not where, making enough noise to strongly suggest that he would be there for a while.

Gunner braved a few seconds to catch his breath before fumbling around for, and finding, a light switch. In the well-diffused glow of two ceramic table lamps at opposite ends of Sheila's front room, their bulbs unguarded by shades, the wiry man on the floor beside the couch was everything Gaines had said he would be: of medium height, slim, and no fighter. Ray Hollins, Sheila's friend from the Motor City, was out cold.

Sheila herself was nowhere in sight. Gunner frisked Hollins quickly for weapons and scanned the floor for one the purported pugilist might have lost in the heat of their modest scuffle. Finding nothing, he cast but a casual glance over the mundane decor of the place and set out to find the lady of the house.

There was a bedroom to his left and a kitchen to his right, with a small bathroom in between. He rolled his eyes around in the bathroom for a while, then advanced to the kitchen. It was full of smells he didn't like, smells that had little or nothing to do with cooking. He was reaching for the light switch when someone made a clumsy attempt to sneak up behind him, running without stealth and knocking things over along the way. He needed no clairvoyance to guess who it was, but played it safe and spun around to throw a right hand with something on it, anyway.

Sheila dropped like a stone, a knife the size of a small machete leaving her hand as she fell.

Two women, two right hands. He understood the occasional necessity of the practice, but slapping women around was still nothing he wanted to become proficient at.

Annoyed, he tossed Sheila's knife into the safety of the kitchen and dragged the hooker's limp form across the carpet to the couch, where he parked her parallel to Hollins, who was just now starting to come around. Gunner took a seat on the arm of an overstuffed easy chair and watched him blink a few times, recall where he was and who he was with, and then make a shaky move to get up.

"You don't want to do that," Gunner said, smiling the smile of a new friend.

Hollins took his advice and relaxed, until catching sight of Sheila for the first time. She had turned to one side, away from him, and her resemblance to a corpse was a strong one.

Hollins started to cry.

"Shit, man," he said, his lips barely moving. "You *killed* her!"

Sheila belched in her sleep. She rolled over toward him and opened her eyes, showing him all the white around her irises.

"How're you doing, Sheila?" Gunner said.

The sound of his voice drove her, backpedaling, up against Hollins and the base of the couch. She stared at the detective blankly, failing to recognize him right away.

"Aaron?"

"Yeah. Long time no see, huh?"

She kept her guard up, refusing to relax, and rubbed her left cheek, saying nothing.

"You're probably wondering why I'm here," Gunner said, smiling again.

"You the one that hit me?"

"Yeah. You were the one with the knife, right?"

She tried to remember, did, and nodded. "I didn't know it was you. I thought it was somebody else."

"I figured as much."

She sat up, struck with a sudden thought. "What *are* you doing here?" she asked, reaching for Hollins's hand.

Gunner said, "I thought maybe you could use a few dollars. In exchange for a small favor."

"Who the hell are you?" Hollins demanded. He had been taking in their exchange with exemplary patience up to now.

Gunner tossed him a glance of unmistakable disrespect. "An old friend."

"He's okay, honey," Sheila said, squeezing the young man's hand, watching the tears dry to salty streaks on his face. "This is Aaron. Aaron Gunner. He's an old drinkin' buddy of mine. We got what you call a 'plutonic relationship.'"

"Strictly," Gunner agreed, nodding.

Hollins didn't say anything. Sheila turned to Gunner and said, "What kind of favor you want? Not the usual kind, I know."

Gunner smiled weakly and shook his head, hoping she wasn't warming up to another big come-on, Hollins or no Hollins. "I need to ask you a few questions, Sheila. About the man who killed J.T. and Buddy Dorris at the Deuce."

A long pause. "Why?"

"Because I'm working again. For Buddy's sister, Verna. You know Verna?"

"Never heard of her."

"That's all right. It's not important."

"I thought you gave that shit up, private detectin'. You were supposed to be workin' in construction with your cousin, I thought."

She was on guard again. A private investigator was, after all, a man other people paid to do their dirty work.

"I was. I am. But this came up a few days ago, and I thought I'd give it one more try. For old times' sake."

"You lookin' for the white boy?"

"Yeah." He came right out with it. "And Howard

Gaines says you might be able to tell me where to find him."

Sheila released her grip on Hollins's hand.

"Howard needs to shut the fuck up," Hollins said.

Gunner glowered at him, but made no move from his chair. He didn't want to see the Motown Wonder cry again. He turned to Sheila and asked, "Can you help me, Sheila?"

"Why would I know where you can find him?"

Gunner shrugged. "Maybe because you're a popular girl. One who's been known to go through the phone book looking for tricks, when times are rough. A girl meets a lot of interesting people that way. Black people, white people—you know."

"I don't do much white business," she said.

"So maybe you know him from somewhere else."

Sheila was silent.

Gunner sighed. Whatever Del was doing right now at a fifteen-dollar-an-hour-clip, it couldn't be as difficult as this. "You think *he* sent me, is that it?"

Sheila remained silent.

"You think he called me out of retirement so I could come over here to hold a rap session in your living room. Lay you out, prop you up against the sofa, and wait for you and your boyfriend to come around before knocking you off. That what you think?"

Sheila stared at him, saying nothing. She was holding Hollins's hand again.

"I don't *know* what to think," she said finally. "I'm too damn *scared* to think!"

She scrambled to her feet and followed her nose to a decanter of what Gunner figured to be cheap Scotch sitting along with several short glasses on a table nearby. She poured herself a drink and slammed it down her throat like a dose of castor oil she was afraid to get a good taste of.

"I've been goin' crazy in here," she said, to anyone listening.

"Where do you know the white boy from, Sheila?"

"I've been in this house since the night it happened, waitin' for that crazy sonofabitch to come get me! Ain't been out to work, to party, to play—*nothin'*. He saw my face, he knows who I am!"

"You don't know that," Hollins said, making a valiant stab at manly reassurance. "Just 'cause you recognized him, that don't mean he recognized you."

"Where do you know him from?" Gunner asked again, exasperated.

The hooker poured herself another drink and tugged at the fabric of the cheap kimono she was wearing, making an effort to pull herself together. "He works at a gas station me and Ruth used to stop in at back when Ruth was drivin' her old man's Benz," she said, nursing the Scotch this time. "You remember Ruth—the big girl with the scars where a john cut her up for buyin' a dog? It's an ARCO station, I think. On Figueroa, out by the Coliseum."

"Next to a hamburger stand."

"Yeah. That's the one. We used to go in there after workin' the crowd at Raider games on Sundays, and it used to kill that boy to see us in that Mercedes. He didn't talk much, but you could tell he was a nigger-hater just by the way he pumped your gas. We used to make him wash the windows just to piss him off."

"You get his name?"

"It was on his shirt, but I never paid it any attention. He got mine, though. First name, last name, and middle initial."

"How's that?"

"Last time I seen him there—last December, I think it was—we had an argument. Ruth had him fill the tank, then couldn't pay him. She didn't have any cash. I had a credit card, but he wouldn't take it. He said we'd have to come up with the cash or he was gonna go get a hose and siphon

Ruth's tank. I said bullshit, he was gonna take my card or kiss his gas good-bye. A perfectly good Visa card, took me two years to get one, and he wouldn't honor it! Took it out of my hand and threw it across the lot, laughin' like it was funny or somethin'.

"Well, you know me. I started to go off on the fool, but Ruth wouldn't let me out the car. She says, 'Sheila, baby, this white boy's crazy,' and when I looked at him again, good, I could see she was right. He *wanted* me to try somethin'. So we just split. Left the card and everything. Got the gas, though."

She smiled, thankful for small victories.

"The night he came into the Deuce, I didn't recognize him right away, 'til all the shootin' was over and he looked straight at me." She drew imaginary circles around her left eye with an index finger. "Ain't but so many people with an eye like he's got," she said. "That, and his voice, gave him away. When he said, 'The Brothers of Volition can go fuck themselves,' man, that was it. I knew it was him."

"Was that all he said?"

"Just before he ran out, yeah. Right, baby?"

She looked at Hollins. Totally uninterested, he nodded his head.

"Did he come specifically to kill Buddy, do you think? Or was he just trying to rob the place, and got jumpy?"

"He never asked for no money," Sheila said, shaking her head. "He just came in, told Buddy he was lookin' for him, and blew him away. He could've sat anywhere that night, but he sat next to Buddy. He didn't *want* no money, you ask me."

"It was cold-blooded," Hollins said, his eyes suddenly filled with the memory.

"Lilly seems to think he was after J.T.," Gunner said, just for the hell of it.

Sheila laughed. The two women found each other pretty funny, apparently.

"She would," Sheila said, filling her glass again. "She

probably don't wanna believe it was an accident, her losin' the only man brave enough to climb up on her ass two nights a week."

Gunner stood up and laughed along with her. Hollins joined them not long after.

Mean Sheila could be as mean as the next lady, when she wanted to be.

4

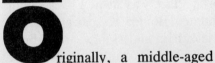riginally, a middle-aged white man in a three-piece suit, eating an Egg McMuffin while reading the back page of the *Wall Street Journal,* had been sitting at the McDonald's booth to Gunner's right, minding his own business. But then the giant black kid wearing corduroy pants and a football jersey with the sleeves torn off asked him to move. In so many words.

"Get your white motherfuckin' ass out the way," he said, looking down over his tray at the poor fellow in pinstripes.

The white man looked to Gunner for help. Gunner pretended not to notice, and the white man retreated without further delay. Gunner wondered if the morning's edition of the *Journal* had run a few lines on the four Caucasian gentlemen who had been beaten close to death on a crowded bus in Pittsburgh, late Wednesday.

"You like that, brother?" the kid asked Gunner, grinning as he eased into his new seat.

"Not much," Gunner said, impassive, finishing off his coffee.

"I'm ready for the war, see. That's what I am. You ready for the war, Home?"

The kid lifted the front of his jersey up to expose the taped and retaped hilt of an old handgun, jammed down into the waistband of his pants. His grin was electric, if not altogether whole.

"I've already had my war," Gunner said, standing up.

"Yeah," the kid said, covering the gun up again. "But this one gonna be ours, Home. This one gonna be *ours* . . ."

He laughed and watched Gunner race a brace of giggling high schoolers to the nearest door.

The ARCO gas station on the corner of Figueroa and 41st Place was owned by a middle-aged Armenian refugee named Boulos Kasparian. He was a short little man with dark hair and skinny arms, bushy eyebrows, and a beard that seemed stunted in its growth. He had dirt under his fingernails and grease stains on his clothes, sure signs of a man with a solid work ethic, but the frailty of his body made him look as if his muscles had never been tested by labor of any kind.

Wednesday night, only minutes after leaving Mean Sheila in the incapable hands of Ray Hollins, Gunner had come to Kasparian's place of business looking for a man allegedly under his employ, a man who was either a murderer or a murderer's near twin, but an articulate black teenage girl manning the gas pumps had denied any knowledge of such an individual, professionally or otherwise, and had recommended Gunner speak with the boss. Kasparian was off on Wednesdays, she said, try early Thursday.

Early Thursday by Gunner's standards was a few minutes past eleven the next day, and not long after his encounter with the black urban guerrilla at McDonald's and the worst fast-food breakfast he had ever scraped off a

Styrofoam plate, he pulled his car onto the lot, beyond the empty service islands up to the open garage bay door, feeling like he had risen with the sun. The girl in the clean blue uniform he had spoken to previously was again on duty, stocking a wavering metal rack with cans of oil in front of the station's office window, but Kasparian himself walked out of the garage to assist him, wiping grime from his hands with a rag as he approached.

"Nice car," he said.

Gunner had just stepped out of a fire engine red Ford Shelby Cobra, circa 1965, an aluminum-bodied, two-passenger missile that could dismantle virtually anything the state of California allowed on public streets. It *was* a nice car.

"Thanks," Gunner said.

"You want to sell?"

"No."

"I give you good price. I have brother-in-law in restoration business. He would pay very good money for car like this."

"I bet he would. Mr. Kasparian?"

Kasparian nodded warily, fearing an unsolicited sales pitch. Gunner offered the smaller man his hand and introduced himself. He opened his wallet to show Kasparian his faded license and the Armenian glanced at it just to be polite.

"Very nice," Kasparian said.

Gunner described the man he was looking for, stressing the point of a bad eye with a zigzagging finger aimed at one of his own, and asked Kasparian if the description fit anyone he knew. Walking around the Cobra like a lion circling its next meal, inspecting detail, Kasparian wasn't listening. Like most people, he couldn't see a hard-luck black man like Gunner coming by the car's pink slip legitimately.

"You have car long?" he asked.

"Seventeen years. It was a gift."

An inheritance is what it was. Some reckless red-neck

kid fresh off the sands of Myrtle Beach, South Carolina, had willed it to him almost gladly—but he had had to step on a fragmentation mine in Da Nang before he felt so inclined.

The car was all Gunner had left to remind him of Duke all in one piece.

With some annoyance, Gunner put the question to Kasparian again, less cordially—did he know a white man with a jittery left eye?—and this time, Kasparian answered it.

"I know who you are looking for," he said, nodding. He walked back around to the detective's side of the car and stayed put. "You are looking for Denny. Denny Townsend. He work here on weekends and Wednesdays, until I fire him three months ago, almost. A crazy man. Good for trouble, only."

Gunner pulled the notebook and Lilly's pen from his pocket. "Spell that last name," he said.

"Townsend. T-O-W-N-S-E-N-D, Townsend. He is sick in the head, I think. He has problem with people." He looked at Gunner sheepishly. "*Black* people. And I figure, this is wrong neighborhood for that kind of problem, right? Somebody with that kind of problem here, in this neighborhood, is going to get hurt one day, or hurt somebody else, right? Is unevitable, I figure."

"Inevitable," Gunner said.

"Inevitable, yeah. So I fire him, three months ago. What did he do? He kill somebody, I bet?"

Gunner didn't see any point in lying about it. "Somebody who looked like him did. You wouldn't happen to have his address?"

Kasparian nodded, and Gunner sent him off to the office to look for it. The detective watched the black girl working the islands wash the windshield of an old green Volkswagen Beetle while waiting for the station owner's return. She was carefully scraping a mosquito carcass off the glass with a long fingernail, under the guidance of a shirtless, tanned beach bum behind the wheel. The hamburger stand next door was filling the air hovering over the block with the distinct odors of grease and mayonnaise, and Gunner turned toward it; a bronze BMW with an odd combination of wheels—three gleaming *Enkei* mags and one stock rim—was sitting beside a drive-through window, its driver impossible to see beyond the car's darkly tinted glass.

Later, pressing the Cobra north on Rossmore Avenue toward nine famous white letters sitting on the face of a dungy Hollywood hill, a pink slip of paper with Kasparian's handwriting on it tucked between the pages of the notebook in his pocket, he would think the BMW unimportant.

And fail to see it in his rearview mirror.

Two thousand fifty-four Argyle Avenue was a dump.

It was a dilapidated two-story apartment building near the end of Argyle's steep but truncated climb into the Hollywood Hills, just east of Vine Street and north of Franklin Avenue, above Hollywood Boulevard. Low-cost, multi-unit dwellings were the rage along this stretch of real estate, packed to and beyond their limit with illegal aliens and others in their general tax bracket. Cars of all sizes and shapes, mutilated, discolored, and leaning, lined both sides of the street like wrecks in a junkyard, their grilles—those that had grilles—pointing in a hundred different directions. The apartment buildings themselves were in no better shape. Screens dangled from broken windows by a single nail and stuccoed walls suffered the indignities of cracks and sun-bleached paint; tiny front yards settled for dirt in the absence of grass and gathered more than their fair share of trash.

It wasn't the Hollywood of picture postcards.

Gunner declined to look for a curbside parking space he knew wasn't there and pulled directly into 2054's sub-level lot instead, where the Cobra would be conspicuous but relatively safe from thieves. He drove well to the rear and took a space labeled 206. The slot for apartment 202 was also vacant, several rows away in close proximity to the garage entrance, but it belonged to Denny Townsend, according to Kasparian's note, and Gunner wasn't reckless enough to take it. A fire engine red convertible might not remind Townsend of the law, but it would certainly get his attention were he to stumble upon it, and any change in the local scenery would likely scare him off for good.

If he wasn't gone already.

In the building's lobby, Gunner scrutinized the mailboxes spanning its southern wall and discovered Townsend's name, scribbled almost indecipherably, on a paper label affixed to the box for apartment 202. A good sign. If Townsend had picked up and moved out, he would have done so weeks ago, not just in the last few days, and by now a warm body would have claimed his apartment and the mailbox that went with it. Units like these didn't sit around empty for long, being as they were the closest thing to affordable housing Los Angeles knew how to provide.

A large woman in an overstuffed bathing suit was spread out on a patio chair in the courtyard, dividing her attention between a Harlequin Romance and three children jumping in and out of the putrid water filling the swimming pool. Gunner gave paying a visit to the resident manager some serious thought before taking the stairs up to the second floor and Townsend's apartment. A key to 202 would have been nice to have along, but landlords, judging by his experience, were difficult to bullshit and expensive to buy.

He reached Townsend's door and slipped the .357 Smith & Wesson Police Special inside his coat from its tattered holster under his left arm, resting its weight against his thigh furtively, out of view of the group at the pool downstairs. It was a heavy thing, a black metal relic scarred with age and slowed by abuse, but the holes it tended to put in people were of the debilitating variety, and Gunner liked such a characteristic in a weapon. He wasn't much of a marksman, and reducing return-fire to a minimum was his favorite gunfight tactic.

He peeked furtively in Townsend's window, but there wasn't much to see. The curtains were cracked, but the room beyond was dark and silent. He stepped away from the door and punched the doorbell once with his thumb, waiting. Nothing happened. He thought to ring the bell again, but decided not to; he didn't think Townsend was home. If Sheila's memory for faces could be trusted, the gas station attendant had killed two people and made a few thousand enemies because of it, and no one in his position was going to wait for a black man he didn't know to ring his doorbell twice before making some attempt to defend himself.

Still, Gunner kept the .357 unholstered and tried the door on a whim, remembering how easily Mean Sheila's had flown open in his hand the day before. It was locked. There was no give in it worth noting, which meant he was up against a dead-bolt mechanism.

And that meant he was out of luck.

He was marginally efficient at slipping conventional locks with a credit card or thin strip of celluloid, but dead-bolts were dead ends for novice burglars with bad hands, and playing with this one would just be a waste of his time. Understanding that the giant revolver on his hip could go unnoticed by Townsend's neighbors for only so long, he was about to head downstairs to squeeze the landlord for a key when inspiration embraced him and he returned to the window instead, clutching at straws. It turned out to be a good move.

The frame of Townsend's window was the same one Gunner had seen a million times before, an engineering marvel of function and frugality unparalleled in its almost total disregard for security. At either end of a fixed pane, a pair of glass rectangles ran along common rails above and below, sliding east and west to open and close. They were closed now, but the aluminum clamps that should have been fastened to the upper rail to obstruct their movement were missing, replaced by a typical, insufficient alternative:

a long wooden dowel sitting snugly between the guides of the bottom rail. It was Gunner's experience that the dowel did its job fairly well when it was the proper diameter and cut to an appropriate length, but when it was an inch too short and a quarter of an inch too fat for the width of the lower rail to fully accommodate . . .

Gunner slapped the window's fixed pane with an open hand once, near the bottom rail, and the dowel disappeared, rolling over the edge of the inner sill, down to the floor below.

Gunner grinned.

He pulled the small screen closest to the door away from the window frame, overpowering the stripped threads of two short screws, threw the screen into the apartment, and slipped through the window after it, looking back over his shoulder to see whether anyone was watching. No one was.

Obviously, Townsend's apartment building was a crime wave waiting to happen.

Gunner set the screen behind a couch bleeding white stuffing, closed the window behind him, and moved directly to the apartment's bedroom, showing the small and impersonal living room only rudimentary interest as he navigated his way through it. A psychologist adept at interpreting trash might have been able to read something of importance into the furnishings, but to Gunner they were just a testimonial to Townsend's fondness for Coors in cans and the *Los Angeles Times* funny pages.

The bedroom, on the other hand, was nothing less than an inanimate extension of the man himself. Who he was and how he lived was here an open book, a mystery revealed like the workings of a pocket watch exposed to the naked eye. Whereas the living room was nondescript, devoid of decoration, this room was flamboyant, a prime example of interior graphics run amok. A water bed bearing a single, shocking-pink sheet sat in the middle of the floor, surrounded on three sides by an uncoordinated mix of poster art Scotch-taped to the walls. The posters covered a wide variety of subjects, from women in compromising modes of undress to soldiers at war, but viewed as a whole they could be seen to adhere to a common theme of ultra-conservative politics and dedication to all things white, people most especially.

Townsend didn't know it, but he was being redundant, for the huge Confederate flag engulfing the far wall opposite the bedroom door was all the delineation his sympathies required. Gunner could recite the values Old Glory tended to stand for from memory, and like most men with ancestral ties to the casualties of slavery, he didn't share many of them.

The black man went over the room quickly, not using his hands when his eyes alone would do. A small library of pornographic magazines lay on the floor beside the bed, the kind that made no effort to be anything more than smut. Soiled underwear was tossed about freely, like seeds Townsend had sown to the wind and was expecting to take root in the carpet. Empty beer cans were again in abundant supply, but in an assortment of brands, Coors being predominant. A drab J.C. Penney wardrobe took up very little space in an open closet, a few pieces of denim and corduroy dangling from misshapen wire hangers over two pairs of athletic shoes.

Some generic toiletries stood atop a tiny dresser in one corner, assembled in disarray around a cheap watch, a dirty ceramic ashtray, and a cardboard box filled with "Henshaw for Congress" campaign buttons. Lew Henshaw was Townsend's type of people, to be sure: he was a former Chicago cop running on a law-and-order platform that appealed to every God-fearing paranoid schizophrenic in the district armed with the right to vote. Mixed in with the buttons was a green Henshaw flyer with a phone number scribbled across the back; no name or address to go with it, just a number.

Without knowing why, Gunner slipped the flyer into

his pocket and was sifting through a drawer stuffed with dirty socks when a key started working on the lock of the apartment door.

He nudged the dresser drawer closed and scanned the room for points of exit. There were two doors and a window, but the window didn't count, leading as it did to nothing but air thirty feet off the ground. The doors led to the bathroom and the living room, respectively, which left him with a choice that was no choice at all, between confrontation and retreat. Confrontation was acceptable if Townsend was out there alone, but if he had company a tête-à-tête would be messy. Gunner went with retreat and made fast tracks for the bathroom.

The apartment door opened and closed out in the living room as the black man stepped into the bathtub to hide, the primitive .357 once more filling his hand. Having left but a crack of an opening at the bathroom door, he stood behind the camouflage of darkness and the mildewed glass of the tub's shower partition and hoped he was harder to see from the bedroom than he felt.

A vaguely human shape appeared at the bedroom doorway and only then did Gunner wonder what, if anything, he had done with the screen to the living room window.

The figure at the door came hesitantly forward. Specifics were indiscernible but generalities were not difficult to make out. It was a man, dark-haired and clean-shaven, fat in all the wrong places for a man and too short to disguise it, wearing something yellow that made him look like a giant egg yolk. Splinters of light kept bouncing off of something in his hand. There was a chance it was Townsend underneath all the mass he seemed to be carrying, but it wasn't a good one; his walk was a fat man's walk, slow and indignant, a gait few men of moderate weight could mimic, and his mannerisms were those of a stranger to his surroundings. The big man poked his head into the closet for a moment, then continued on, toward the bathroom and the detective in it. He stopped short of the door and peered in, giving the room a long, hard look. The thing in his hand was a gun.

Abruptly, the bathroom lost his interest and he turned away from the door, stepping out of Gunner's sight. He started to ransack the dresser, and Gunner didn't have to see him to know it; he was making noise now, satisfied that he had Townsend's apartment to himself. When he had pulled the last of six drawers open and picked through its contents thoroughly, he took up a new occupation, one not easily identified by sound alone. He was rattling something. The box of campaign buttons. Grabbing a handful.

Or searching for something among them.

He made a mess of the toiletries atop the dresser, sounding frustrated, and returned to Gunner's field of vision, dropping a small pile of clothes upon Townsend's bed. He snatched two pairs of pants and a shirt from the closet and added them to his collection, then pulled the case from the bed's lone pillow and began to stuff the clothes into it.

He was packing an overnight bag.

The big man tied a hasty knot in the pillowcase and ran out, into the living room. The apartment door closed behind him and Gunner scrambled out of the bathroom to follow him, the Police Special still in his closed right fist.

Down on the street, Townsend's portly friend got into an old converted U.S. Postal Service jeep parked across a driveway and started it up on the fourth try. He turned the jeep away from the curb and Gunner's red Cobra slid furtively out of shadow into light from the parking lot of Townsend's building, coasting patiently down Argyle in the jeep's wake, letting it take a lead it had no prayer of keeping if push came to shove.

And high on top of the hill, far above them both, a bronze BMW with one oddball wheel fell quietly into line behind them.

It wasn't much of a chase, as it developed. The fat man in the jeep treated Gunner to a short tour of Hollywood

Boulevard before finding a place to park near the Hollywood YMCA on Hudson and Selma, a mere mile from Townsend's apartment. Gunner parked the Cobra one block farther east on Selma and pretended not to notice Townsend's courier heave a stuffed pillowcase over one shoulder, mount the short stairs to the Y, and disappear inside.

Gunner was at least casually familiar with several other local chapters of the YMCA and found them all pretty much alike, but the Hollywood club was unique in ways he was able to sense from the front desk, where a sinewy young man with an expensive coiffeur charged him six dollars for use of the facilities. The air was buried in the customary stench of sweat, and far-off weight machines clanked their accompaniment to the squeal of tennis shoes dueling on a basketball court, but there was an inoffensive flavor to it all that had no place in such surroundings. The Y was supposed to be an arena where men went to wage war in the civilized guise of sportsmen, but there were no real battles being fought here, only polite skirmishes drawing no blood, full of raised voices woefully lacking conviction. Gunner recognized the feel of the place as that of Hollywood's less infamous persona, the flip side to its overblown image as the Black Kingdom of homicide and vice. This was Tinseltown under the harsh light of truth, unflattering and not very sensational.

Neutered. Harmless. Tame.

Three doors surrounded the Y's service desk, leading into various parts of the club, and Gunner had no choice but to pick one at random, as the man toting Townsend's goods, a giant in a yellow windbreaker that would have made him stand out in the sea of fans at a World Series game, was nowhere in sight. Gunner chose the door closest to the desk, off the long hallway he had traversed to get here, and the attendant toed a button on the floor to buzz him in.

Climbing a long flight of stairs immediately on his

right, the detective came upon the door to a weight room and peered in. Four men who seemed to have cornered the market on muscle tissue were pumping iron for the edification of their reflections in various mirrored walls, while a Hispanic teenager in shorts three sizes too large for his spindly frame tried to figure out how to work a Nautilus leg machine. None of them even remotely resembled the fat man in the windbreaker.

He moved well for a big man, apparently.

Gunner gave the rest of the second floor a cursory inspection, pausing to look over the diverse inhabitants of two basketball courts, four handball courts, an aerobics room, and two additional free-weight stations, but at tour's end only found himself with yet another difficult decision to make: what to do now? He could either go back down the stairs to try the other two doors off the service desk, or proceed onward and upward, to the third floor and, if possible, whatever points lay beyond.

He stood at the landing of the staircase leading skyward and studied its ascent. It looked like a steep climb he didn't want to make, and that, he decided, was probably how the fat man would have felt about it, too. He retraced his steps and tried a new door on the first floor below.

Bingo.

Townsend's heavy friend was in the locker room, spinning the dial of a combination padlock securing one of the lockers in the back, struggling to perform a task too delicate for his meaty fingers to pull off with any grace. The sounds of male horseplay betrayed the presence of two other men in the room with him, but they were off in a distant corner and he was ignoring them accordingly.

Gunner's arrival, however, he found distracting. At the sound of the door ringing open, he looked up from the lock to watch the black man come in, by all appearances just another jock looking for a place to change. The detective turned into the bathroom nearby, groping for the fly of his pants, and disappeared inside. The fat man took a deep breath and went back to work.

The jaws of the lock popped free. He snatched the locker door open, exchanged a bulky envelope inside for the loaded pillowcase, then secured the locker again, spinning the padlock's dial to make sure it was closed for good. He peeled the envelope open for a brief instant—lifting a few crisp bills out for a close look—and smiled.

Standing at a urinal in the bathroom, going through the motions of relieving himself, Gunner used the full-length mirror in the other room to watch the big man shove the envelope into his windbreaker's left-hand pocket and leave, glancing half-heartedly from side to side to look for a witness he didn't want to see.

Gunner was tempted to follow, but not much.

Waiting for Townsend to come get his clothes was no sure thing, but unless the white boy had more between his ears than the thin air people gave him credit for, it was a risk worth taking. Townsend had paid someone good money to assemble a CARE package and drop it here at the Y, and sooner or later, either in person or by yet another proxy, he was going to show up to retrieve it.

Gunner found an empty locker along the same row as Townsend's and slipped quickly out of his coat and shoulder holster. He didn't want to be standing around twiddling his thumbs when the white man made his entrance, and taking his shirt and shoes on and off before a vacant locker seemed like a clever way to look busy at any given moment.

He tossed his coat into the locker atop the holster, followed that with his shirt, and bent down to untie a shoe. The same pair of male voices he had heard earlier wandered toward the door, and Gunner glanced up just long enough to watch two middle-aged white men in matching raquetball togs and headbands leave the room. He turned his head before the door closed behind them, pulled his left shoe off and threw it in with the rest, then went to work on the right.

The laces never came loose in his hands.

Something very unforgiving collided with the base of his skull and he hit the concrete floor with his face, meeting the black wall of unconsciousness head-on, without resistance.

He was sitting on a hard toilet seat when he next opened his eyes. Somebody had propped him up in the far stall where he wouldn't easily be discovered, still naked from the waist up. He blinked twice, hard, and forced himself upright and mobile. He stumbled into a short, naked man on his way to the urinals, bounced off him into the locker room and came to a halt on wavering legs in front of Townsend's locker. The lock on the door was open; the pillowcase full of clothes was still inside. A half-dozen lockers down, his shoulder holster lay empty atop his shirt and coat.

Gunner fell twice trying to run to his car outside. He felt sick all the way there, and worse when he finally made it. A man with filthy blond hair sat slumped over in the Cobra's passenger seat, his head resting awkwardly against the dashboard. He could have been asleep, but he wasn't; there was a hole in him somewhere, Gunner knew, and a .357 Police Special had most likely made it.

Mean Sheila had nothing more to fear from the white boy with the funny left eye.

And neither would anyone else, ever again.

Detective Lieutenant Matthew Poole of the Los Angeles Police Department, Homicide Division, blew the steam from a cup of hot coffee and said, "You're never gonna guess who we found dead yesterday."

He tried the coffee and watched Gunner's face project indifference. It wasn't the best blank mug he had ever seen, but it deserved an honorable mention.

"Yeah?"

"White guy by the name of Denny Townsend. *The* Denny Townsend."

"*The* Denny Townsend."

"Yeah. The one you've been lookin' for for the last few days. That Denny Townsend."

"Oh, right, right. *That* Denny Townsend." Gunner nodded his head, seeming to remember something long forgotten. "He's dead, huh?"

Poole nodded, dropping another cube of sugar into his

cup. "Somebody shot him in the midsection with a high-caliber handgun and left his body in a dumpster behind the Newberry's on Western and Venice. He got it somewhere between the hours of one and four P.M. Thursday, the coroner figures."

"Damn."

"Yeah. That's what I said."

"Any witnesses?"

Poole shook his head. "Uh-uh."

He drank some more coffee and dropped a good spot of it on the solid green tie he was wearing. The stain it created wasn't going to be lonely there: it was but the latest addition to an already expansive collection, mementos of culinary exploits past.

But then, stains went well with Poole. He was a slow man in his late forties whose body looked like a suit he had slept in; it was a loose jumble of flesh and bone, of formidable dimension but completely unintimidating. He had a basset hound's swaying jowls and more straight black hair than he knew how to comb.

Perhaps to compensate, he kept a fairly clean, upbeat cubicle in the otherwise decadent 77th Street Station building near Broadway. The city had actually coughed up a few dollars for partitions to block off one detective's floor space from another's, and Poole was cornered at the far end of the squad room where the window blinds were open to the sun's advances and the walls were patched and freshly painted. There was even a potted Boston fern hanging from the ceiling, in good health and thriving.

"Why aren't you surprised?" Poole asked Gunner, mopping his tie with a coat sleeve. "Don't tell me you already knew?"

"Day-old news is old news, Lieutenant. You want to surprise people, do card tricks."

"Bet your client's all messed up about it, huh?"

"Actually, I haven't seen her since I heard, so I can't say. But I imagine she's taking it pretty well."

"I don't suppose you'd know who did the dirty deed?"

Gunner didn't like the chair he was sitting in; it was hard and uncomfortable, designed to make interrogations a miserable experience. "Like any good citizen, I would have come forward if I did."

"You could make an educated guess," Poole said.

"You dragged me in here to make an educated guess? Okay. How's this: it was somebody black. Sympathetic to the Brothers of Volition and pissed about what happened to Buddy Dorris. Does that narrow the field down any for you?"

"You think Townsend killed Buddy Dorris?"

"I didn't say that. I don't know if he did or not; I never caught up to the man to ask him. But he fit the bill, and was making himself hard to find for some reason."

"Was he?"

"Yeah. He was." Gunner had no trouble following Poole's train of thought. "Like I said, I never caught up to the man."

Poole let the expression on his face say how much he believed that, but didn't press the issue. "How'd you come to be looking for Townsend in the first place? You pick up his scent all by yourself, or did somebody steer you his way?"

Guardedly, Gunner said, "I was steered."

"By who?"

"I'd rather not say."

"Oh, yeah?"

"Yeah."

Poole sipped his coffee, then asked, "Need a few days of peace and quiet to change your mind?"

"Look, don't give me that bullshit, Poole. It doesn't make any difference who steered me his way, all right?"

Poole watched Gunner squirm about in the hard wooden chair and laughed at his little joke. Poole was no good at playing the tough cop—the hardline dialogue fell off his tongue like a lead weight. He could fake it from time to time on a sucker new to the territory, but practicing on Gunner was an embarrassing mistake. The black man knew him too well.

"Okay, okay," the lieutenant said. "Let me rephrase the question. Anybody else looking for Townsend that you know of?"

"Not for him specifically, no. But the streets have been crawling with people looking for the guy who killed Buddy Dorris, and maybe that's the same thing, and maybe it isn't. You think I'm the only one to notice Townsend had a bad left eye?"

Poole shrugged. "Probably not. But you're the only one I've got. And you know what they say—a bird in the hand . . ."

He was a fair man, Poole, but not one gifted with a lot of perseverance when it came to breaking cases; any slob he could get the shoe to fit was all right by him, ninety percent of the time.

"Kiss my ass, Lieutenant. You don't *have* a bird in your hand."

Poole smiled at him.

"Why would *I* want to kill the sonofabitch? All I had to do to earn my money was turn him over to you."

"Or just point your nose in his direction."

"I don't work like that anymore," Gunner said.

"But you used to. All the time."

Gunner shook his head. "Not anymore."

"Not even for close personal friends? I hear you and the lady paying your bills are like this." He pressed the first two fingers of his right hand together and held them up in the air.

Gunner said, "You don't hear anything, Poole. That's your problem. You can't get enough of your own voice, how're you going to hear anyone else's?"

Poole laughed again and sat down, stretching out in the chair behind his desk luxuriously. "Yeah, you're right," he said, popping a stick of gum into his mouth. "We don't have to go through all this shit. I had the answers to my questions three hours before you got here. I'm just talking to you for the exercise."

He popped his gum for Gunner's benefit, his teeth working industriously behind a John Doe smile. "Take the name of your client, for example. If I were to ask you who you're working for, you'd say a fine young thing by the name of Verna Gail, Dorris's big sister, because you haven't exactly been making it a secret and you'd figure that's something I already know. And then, if I were to wonder where you were between the hours of one and four P.M. Thursday, you'd tell me about the dynamite book you took all day to read, tucked between the sheets of your bed at home with no one around to interrupt. Right? Am I right?"

Gunner was silent.

Poole laughed again. "Uncanny, isn't it, how a dumb-shit cop like me always seems to know these things?"

"Uncanny," Gunner agreed, dourly. "You ought to get yourself an agent, Lieutenant."

"An agent? Naw. An agent would want me to take my act out on the road. Do Vegas, Atlantic City—go on a world tour, maybe. And that's not for me. I'm just a simple joe, trying to make a living in a crazy world—same as you.

"I mean, hell, I don't want to pin Townsend's murder on you, Gunner. You didn't kill anybody, I know that. So what if some grease monkey at an ARCO station says he gave you directions to Townsend's place? So what if we did lift a few of your prints off the "can" in his bathroom? That's no kind of evidence to take a man in on. Especially if the rap's murder-one."

He sat up in his chair and lowered his voice to something just above a whisper. "Trouble is, like I said, you're all I've got. And a lot of people I know, people I work for, in fact, would say you're more than good enough. Good enough for the department, good enough for the D.A."

"But you don't want to turn me over to the D.A.," Gunner said, glaring at Poole with open contempt.

"No. Nobody's turning the screws yet, why should I? For a few hours, at least, I've got time. Time to sit back, look around, and maybe find the real McCoy. That would be a kick, wouldn't it?"

"It'd be a *first*, is what it would be."

"Okay. Maybe so. But it's the only shot you've got at spending your next twenty birthdays on the street, my man, and that's straight from the fucking heart. Because unless somebody better comes along fast, I'm gonna make like a tailor and try Townsend's murder on you for size. And if it fits, it fits. Case closed. You read me, brother?"

"Tell me what you want, Poole. Say it and get it over with, for Chrissake."

"I want some *help*, goddammit. That's what I want. I want to do the right thing, for once. Race relations in this country are the worst they've been in twenty-five years, and the heat's driving everyone in this city nuts. Maybe it hasn't exactly been this department's policy to bust the *right* black people for homicides up to now, but I figure this is as intelligent a time to start as any. Because Townsend *did* kill Buddy Dorris—we found the murder weapon in the dumpster with his body—and whoever killed *him* is gonna be one hell of a popular guy with your people when we make an arrest.

"We grab the wrong guy, and anything could happen. The Fire Next Time, maybe. And I don't want that on my conscience, such as it is."

Gunner shrugged. "So?"

"So go home and make up your mind what you want to be for the rest of your life. An electrician or a private detective. You want to be an electrician, stay in bed and relax for a couple of days; another black-and-white'll be dropping by the pad, sooner or later, to bring you in for good. You want to be a detective, on the other hand, start doing what detectives do and save your ass."

He smiled, smacking his gum again. "You've got seventy-two hours. After that, you're A.P.B. meat."

Gunner stood up. "Am I supposed to say thanks, or something?"

Poole said, "You're supposed to be a cop, for once in your life. Think you can do that?"

Gunner was halfway out of the cubicle when Poole called him back. "Oh, before I forget—just thought I'd ask—you still use that elephant gun you used to carry? The Special?"

Gunner shook his head. "Had to sell it some time back. To buy something frivolous like food, I think."

The homicide detective got a big kick out of that, his gum flying around in his mouth like a numbered ball in a keno scrambler. "See? I did it again. I *knew* you were gonna say somethin' like that."

Gunner mumbled something deliberately unintelligible and walked away.

6

Verna Gail had an apartment in a clean little building on Budlong Avenue between Century and Imperial, a late-model fortress with bars on the windows and a security gate, but nobody answered back when Gunner used the intercom out front to buzz her first-floor unit. For the third straight day, he tried it several times, forcing himself to be patient, but it didn't get him anywhere; if he had any friends inside, they weren't making it known.

It was Saturday. The Cobra had been out of the downtown storage garage he normally kept it in for three days now, and it needed a wash. The passenger seat would never be the same; Townsend's blood was still in the leather, though the stains it left behind after Gunner's vigorous scrubbing could no longer be easily recognized for what they were, barring forensic scrutiny. There was a car wash a few blocks away on Imperial at Normandie, but Gunner drove past it to the Church's Fried Chicken stand on the opposite corner and dialed Verna's number from a phone in the parking lot. The line wasn't busy; as it had Thursday night and all day Friday, it rang in his ear like a broken alarm clock. He slapped the receiver back onto its cradle and tried something different, something, in retrospect, he should have tried sooner: he flipped through a dilapidated copy of the phone book for a listing for Buddy Dorris.

There were only two full pages of the "D" section left intact, but Buddy was on one of them: beside the name *Dorris, Bud L.* was an address falling along the 9200 block of Holmes Avenue on the edge of Watts, followed by a phone number Gunner started to dial, then decided not to use. He butchered the page ripping it out of the book and stuffed it into his pocket, reducing the book's overall range of "D" listings to a certifiably worthless smidgen.

The Cobra had three kids in a freshly primered Chevrolet lowrider bouncing around on their seats as it rolled northbound on Wilmington toward the last home Buddy Dorris would ever know, but Gunner was too caught up in a mire of grim thought to notice, as he had been for the last forty-eight hours.

Somebody had set him up for Denny Townsend's murder, and they hadn't done it just to see a funny look come over his face. He wanted to believe that he alone was the target of the exercise, that there was a personal vendetta behind the frame that necessitated his specific involvement in it, but he knew that wasn't the case. The objective had been Townsend's execution, pure and simple, and Gunner had just been one of the tools the job required. Apparently, he was making quite a reputation for himself as a brainless instrument of the psychotic, a prize sucker with the smarts of a good bird dog and the net worth of a disposable razor, and he didn't much like it.

He pushed into Watts and watched the surface of the streets deteriorate with his descent, the white concrete's black tar repair scars playing a staccato beat against rubber as the convertible eagerly crushed them underfoot. To his way of thinking, pavement was as clear an indicator of a community's well-being as anything that rested above it, and the mutilated tarmac maze of south-central Los Angeles was its most glaring badge of insolvency, a readily available reminder of poverty Gunner didn't need, but could never quite ignore. It said something about the ghetto's place in the heart of City Hall, about the great regard elected officials had for the safety and comfort of the poor, and it drove Gunner to review all the other things that were wrong with living on the short side of the dollar. Like cops who snatched men from their homes in the middle of cold showers to see more cops with questions and threats of life imprisonment, or black people who thought nothing of cutting a swath through their own kind just to appease whatever demons they were courting at the moment.

Demons like vengeance, for example.

When Gunner finally found Verna Gail, she was knee-deep in a mess someone else had left behind, in an apartment too small for most men to share with the rodents that lived there, and her frame of mind was not to his liking. He had hoped to find her in high spirits, was counting on a strain or two of her patented acerbic laughter to take his rage up and over the top, to make what he wanted to do a little easier to justify, but the wilted rag doll who failed to greet him at the door wasn't going to be much fun to knock around.

Somebody, it seemed, had tumble-dried the contents of Buddy's apartment, turning everything upside down and bouncing it off the walls for good measure. They hadn't had much furniture to toy with, but what there had been they'd done a good job on. All that was left of it was a shredded couch lying on its back and a few piles of refuse sitting in the middle of the living room, intermingled puzzles with too many missing pieces to count. Record albums, books, a cheap stereo, and a small television were mixed in with the wreckage, mangled fragments of plastic and metal, glass, and newsprint.

It all made for an interesting distraction, but it had nothing to do with why Gunner was here.

Verna was sitting on the skeletal carcass of the over-turned couch when he invited himself in. She was staring at a wall that held nothing of interest to the naked eye but a discolored patch of plaster. Mascara was splashed across her face like war paint and her hair was a jumbled wreck. He tried to wait for her to come around, but it was like waiting for the heat to give up and go away.

"Hey," he said, simply.

She looked up, startled. The orbs of her eyes flashed white in the darkness, lightning against a black summer sky.

"We need to talk," Gunner said.

She looked at him with the same level of interest she had shown for the patch of plaster on the wall, but with considerably less respect. "What are you doing here?" she asked. "I never gave you this address."

"It's in the book. You've been here since Thursday night?"

"I've been in and out. What's it to you?"

"You can't guess?"

"I don't want to guess. And I don't want to talk. Or can't you see I'm a little busy right now?"

He was on top of her before she had a chance to react, drawing her to her feet. The grip he held on her left bicep she wasn't going to break in a lifetime. "This shit can wait. Our business can't. I want to know who killed the white boy for you, Verna. And where I can find him."

"What?"

"You've only got ten seconds. Keep fucking around." Standing only inches from her face, he pulled on her arm, hard.

"I don't know what you're talking about!"

"You told me to my face you'd kill the poor bastard,

and like a moron I shrugged it off. You'd get your chance, you said. Maybe at the trial. Only you weren't up to the wait, were you?"

"No! You're crazy!"

"Crazy's got nothing to do with it! What I am is scared shitless. I've never pulled a day in a state cage and I'm not going to pull any now. Tell me what I want to know, Verna. *Who killed the white boy for you?*"

"Nobody! I didn't even know he was dead!" She jerked away from him all at once, with everything she had, and he allowed her to slip from his grasp. His fingers had left an imprint on her skin, and she stood there working to erase it, her gaze trying to cut him in half.

"*I* wasn't the only friend of Buddy's looking for that white boy! Everybody and their mother was trying to find him. He could've been wasted by anybody!"

Gunner's merciless glare was more than equal to hers. "'Anybody' didn't hire me to take the fall for it. *You* did."

She shook her head, still rubbing her arm. "I hired you to *find* the man, that's all. Not to play you or anybody else for a fool. I'd've put a bullet in his head, given the chance, hell yes, but only if I could take the credit for it. Buddy was *my* brother, not yours.

"Only I never got the chance. You never *gave* me the chance. Because you let somebody else find him *first*—didn't you?"

She laughed, finally, daring him to challenge her right to view him as a joke, and won out. Gunner didn't move.

"But maybe I shouldn't complain. You told me you were lousy, and I wouldn't listen. I thought you were just being modest."

"You're full of shit," Gunner said, reaching for her again.

She backed away, out of his range. "Believe what you want to believe. I've told you what I know, and that's the best I can do for you. If the cops want to think you killed the white boy, that's your problem, not mine."

"Is that right."

"Yeah. That's right. That was you out there beatin' the bushes for him, not me."

"You're confused, sister. And your memory's failing you. I beat the bushes for the man, all right, but I didn't have any motive to kill him. I didn't give a shit about Buddy or the Brothers of Volition, I'm as apolitical as a guy can get. But I've come upon some lean times lately, that's a matter of record, and when some broad with a great body and a fistful of money showed up in my kitchen a few days ago to make me an offer I couldn't refuse . . ."

"What offer? I didn't hire you to kill anybody!"

"Didn't you?"

It was Gunner's turn to laugh. He threw his head back as she came at him with her nails extended, and he caught her wrists, one in each hand, before she could get to his eyes. She thrust a knee up at his groin, but he blocked it with his thigh and shoved her aside, releasing her arms. She backpedaled a few steps and her right hand found the canvas back of a broken director's chair sitting nearby. The chair was up over her head before he could stop her and the best he could do was shield his face with his left forearm as she brought it down on him, putting all her weight behind the blow.

He had been driving himself toward her when the chair disintegrated around his head, and he groped blindly for her throat as his momentum carried him forward, finding her face instead. His left hand held her head in a vise, its fingers splayed wide across her features, as his right looped up to hover, trembling, beside his ear, torqued into a fist coiled to strike.

Verna's eyes shut tight as Gunner let it go.

A framed *Time* magazine cover of the Reverend Jesse Jackson exploded on the wall behind her, just over her left shoulder. She felt a spray of glass shards at the back of her neck and moved away, squinting, no longer bound by his left hand. The frame dropped to the floor like the blade of a guillotine and was still. Gunner's right hand was covered in blood.

He was shaking. She watched him stand there, bleeding profusely, and grimaced. He let her look and said nothing.

"I'm sorry," she said finally, shrugging.

He took a step toward her and brushed the knuckles of his right hand across the yellow front of her blouse, smearing it with blood.

"So am I," he said.

She leaned forward and kissed him, hard. His response was immediate, surprising them both. He was erect when her hand found him, and his breathing was labored, short. He moved his mouth down the nape of her neck and peeled her ruined blouse open, slipping his right hand into the left cup of her bra to ease the full, heavy mound of her breast into the open. The dark flesh of the nipple was hard with arousal even before he brought his lips down around it.

The hand she was using to explore him paused in its vigorous work abruptly, as she lost herself in the playful teasing of his tongue and teeth, and she reached up to free her right breast for him, stroking the nipple to attention with her own hand until he was ready for it. Her breathing, too, had changed its rhythm, dramatically.

"The bedroom," she said, forcefully, and she only had to say it once.

He took her up in his arms and followed her directions to Buddy's bed.

Several hours later, they turned the couch up off its back onto the two legs it had left, retrieved its ravaged cushions from various parts of the room, and sat down to talk. Verna found some beer in the kitchen and brought them both an open bottle. There was no mention of a truce, but that, in effect, was what they were trying. It seemed like the thing to do.

"What happened here?" Gunner asked, surveying the

wreckage of Buddy's apartment. The fresh bandage on his right hand was growing damp with a crimson stain.

Verna sipped her beer and shook her head. "I don't know. A break-in, I guess."

"When?"

"I'm not sure. This is how I found it yesterday morning, the first I'd been here since the night before Buddy died. It could have happened Thursday, or Wednesday—or two weeks ago, for all I know."

"You talk to any of the neighbors? Maybe somebody heard it go down."

"No, I didn't. But I could ask around, I guess."

"Anything missing? Would you know it if there were?"

"You mean like valuables? Money, jewelry—things like that?"

Gunner shrugged. "Anything."

She did a quick inventory of the room, said, "Not that I can tell. What you see is pretty much what he had. A few chairs, some records, a handful of books. That cheap-ass stereo."

"Then they didn't take anything."

"No. I don't think so. Does that mean something?"

Gunner shrugged again. "Probably not."

"Then why all the questions?"

"Force of habit."

"You don't think this was a burglary, do you?"

"It may have started out as a burglary, sure. But thieves don't usually trash a place like this unless . . ."

"Unless what?"

Gunner looked at her. The blood on her blouse had dried a dark brown. "Unless something goes wrong. Something happens to set them off and they take it out on the furniture."

Verna shook her head. "You're not making any sense," she said.

He tasted his beer and let his eyes rest on the bottle's

label, thinking in silence. "I know," he said shortly. "I'm not, am I?"

He downed the bottle in one long, extended swallow and said, "So what do you say we change the subject? To something a little more relevant to our immediate well-being."

She didn't have to be told what, specifically, he had in mind. "The white boy really is dead, huh?"

"Dead. Really. And we're 'as good as' if we don't find out who killed him, providing you or one of your friends didn't."

"Look, how many times do I have to say it? I don't *know* who killed him. I don't know anybody that crazy, or that devoted to Buddy. A few Brothers, maybe, but none of the ones I ever met."

"That include Roland Mayes?"

"Roland? Shit. That goes double for Roland."

"I always thought they were pretty close."

"Yeah. Me, too."

She smiled bitterly and lowered her head. She was rolling her own cold beer bottle around in her hands like a sculptor kneading clay, and began to peer reflectively down its narrow throat.

"They weren't the best of friends?" Gunner asked, pressing.

"Friends? Sure," she said, her head still down. "They were friends. But only barely. And Roland wouldn't kill anybody over a friend. An enemy, maybe. But not a friend."

The subject apparently rubbed her the wrong way; she was getting warmed up again. Her beer was only half-empty, but she flipped the bottle to the cluttered floor anyway, watching it roll to a stop about twenty feet away.

"You get that from Roland himself?" Gunner asked. She seemed not to have heard the question, until she said, "In so many words. I talked to him for about thirty minutes, almost a week before I finally caught up with you. A Wednesday, I think it was, over at that sorry little storefront clubhouse the Brothers have on Vermont, near the USC campus. I wanted to see if they were going to put up any money for a reward, to encourage the community to join in on the hunt for Buddy's murderer. He'd been one of their own; I thought surely they'd have to do something along those lines to save face, to let people know they weren't going to just sit idly by and let a Brother's murder ride.

"But Roland said a reward would be impractical, that their money would be better spent kicking the White Man's ass in Buddy's undying memory. He told me I was being too emotional about it, that the guy who killed Buddy was of more use to the movement as a whole on the loose than he would be dead or in custody, because as long as he was free they could use him as an example of the Man's ineffectual handling of violent crimes against blacks, of our inability to receive fair treatment under the law."

"Not a bad argument," Gunner said, deferentially.

"It was lip service. Bullshit. Those weren't his real reasons for turning me down, and I knew it. He didn't want the Brothers involved in any search for the white boy because that would have been acknowledging the importance of Buddy's death to the movement. He wanted Buddy forgotten, as quickly as possible, and he wasn't about to do anything that would draw more attention to his death than it had already received."

Gunner set his empty beer bottle on the floor between his feet. "That when you suggested hiring somebody like me?"

She brought her head around to face him again, no longer avoiding the weight of his eyes. "Who said I did?"

He shrugged. "If you thought he might put up a few dollars for a reward, you could've also thought he'd cover my fee. Want another beer?"

"No."

Gunner cut a zigzag course through the mine field of the dining room to the kitchen, pulled a fresh beer out of the refrigerator, and quickly returned, twisting the cap off the bottle as he sat back down. He drank some, gave Verna a disapproving look, and drank a little more.

"I guess he didn't think his money would be too well spent, paying a P.I. to look for Townsend."

"He thought it was stupid. He called me an idiot for even suggesting it." She was glaring at him now, her resistance to the memory discarded. "He told me to go home and forget it, because the Brothers weren't going to get off a damn cent for rewards or private cops or anything else I thought the Brothers should finance for Buddy's sake.

"So I told him fine, *I'd* hire somebody; I didn't need his money or his permission to do something for Buddy. I was Buddy's sister, we were one in flesh and blood. But the real bond should have been between Buddy and Roland; they were the ones so attuned to the needs of the people, so hung up on the same, identical revolutionary trip. They had done more and shared more together in the last several years than Buddy and I had our entire lives, but Roland felt no obligation whatsoever to react more forcefully to Buddy's murder. He was content to just let nature take its course, to let the white boy go free so he could make a few more dynamite speeches about the inequities of the legal system and its indifference to black American concerns."

"He had no objection to *your* hiring a private investigator?"

"No."

"Or warn you off the idea, make threats of any kind?"

She shook her head. "He couldn't take me that seriously. He said I could do what I wanted, just as long as I left his and the Brothers' names out of it. I started looking around the next day, and you know the rest."

"Was Roland alone when you talked to him? Or were there other Brothers around at the time?"

"We were alone. Except for Mouse, of course."

Gunner tilted his head curiously to one side.

"Roland's shadow," Verna said. "His bodyguard. At least, that's what I think Mouse is supposed to be." She grinned, picturing him. "He's not big or anything, like most bodyguards you see, but he's crazy. Strange. Never says more than two words to anybody, and he sticks to Roland like glue. I don't know if I've ever seen one without the other."

"And he was there in the room when you talked to Roland."

"Yes. Roland, Mouse, and me. That was it."

"This Mouse have anything to say about your hiring a private cop? Do you remember?"

"Mouse didn't have anything to say about anything. He never does. He just stands there flexing his tight little muscles, hard and skinny and fuzz-headed nigger that he is, and watches. Just watches. That's why they call him Mouse. Quiet as . . ."

"He get along all right with Buddy?"

"As far as I know. They weren't close or anything, but I think they liked each other. Why?"

"I was wondering if maybe Mouse would have cared any more to even the score for Buddy than Roland had."

Verna gave it some thought, then said, "I don't think he's capable of caring for anything more than Roland. Or less."

"Anybody else know your plans, besides Roland and Mouse?"

"What, to hire a private investigator?"

He nodded.

"Not until I actually started asking around for one. But once I did, I imagine quite a few people heard about it, one way or another. Although nobody knew exactly *who* I was going to hire, except maybe Too Sweet, who gave me your name to begin with."

Gunner thought that was pretty funny. *Nobody knew*

except Too Sweet. All one had to do to hear the man's un-
abridged life story was sit two stools down from him at the
bar, any night of the week—but nobody knew except him.

"Have you seen Too Sweet since? Does he know for a
fact that you hired me?"

"No. I only saw him that one time, in Will Rogers
park. But . . ."

"But what?"

"But would it matter? Whether he knows it 'in fact' or
not? Wouldn't he just assume I did?"

"If he could remember talking to you at all. Yeah."

He left his seat on the couch to cross the room and
fished a small plastic trash can out of the rubble on the
floor. He set it upright at his feet and dropped his empty
beer bottle into it, following its descent as if it were a stone
he had fed to a bottomless well.

"So that makes three who knew," he said, still appraising the depths of the little can pensively. *"Only* three."

"Yes."

"You told no one else?"

"No."

"No girl friends, no relatives, no friends of Buddy outside the Brothers' ranks?"

"No. Buddy was all the family I had left, and I don't
trust my business to friends. But *you*—what about *you*?
You spent three days looking for Townsell, right?"

"Two days. It was two days. And the white boy's name
was Townsend, not Townsell."

"Townsend, Townsell, whatever. How many people
did you talk to in two days' time? A dozen? Two dozen?"

It had only been five, but she was making a valid
point. He could just as easily be looking for one of his
friends as one of hers. With a gun in his hand, for instance,
Sheila's beau Ray Hollins didn't have to be quite the wimp
he was without one.

"Who I talked to's my business," Gunner said, trying
to cover his doubt with belligerence. "And who you talked

to is yours. Time's running out, Verna. I've got a lousy forty hours to come up with something, and I may not have that if a certain cop has a sudden change of heart. If you don't know who set me up for the white boy's murder, you can guess."

She shook her head and faced him squarely, letting him see a glimmer of sincerity behind her eyes. "Ask Roland," she said. "Maybe he did do it. I don't know."

Gunner studied her face for a moment. "Where's this clubhouse you were talking about? The Brothers' hangout. On Vermont and what?"

She stood away from the couch and told him, following him over to the apartment's front door. Standing in the hallway, he asked her if her name would be good enough to get him an interview with Mayes.

"If Roland's in a talkative mood," she said.

The hallway was empty, a long garbage chute as devoid of sound as an echo chamber. She watched him stand there from the other side of the open door and said, "About this place. And what they did to it."

"Yeah?"

"You were leading up to something earlier. Like maybe you knew why they wrecked things the way they did."

"It was just a thought," Gunner said.

"Still, I'd like to hear it."

She wasn't going to leave it alone. Gunner took a moment to glance at the ruins of Buddy's apartment one final time. "They were looking for something," he said. "And they didn't find it."

Without waiting to see her reaction, he turned and disappeared down the hall.

unday morning's *Los Angeles Times* was a bad news extravaganza. Temperatures were expected to reach the high nineties for the fourth consecutive day in October, a new record for the city, and no rain was in the forecast. One of two Caucasian policemen responding to a phony rape call had lost an eye to a sniper with a pellet gun in Encino. Weapon sales throughout the L.A. basin were up thirty-five percent from the previous year. And the UCLA Bruins had blown their Pac-10 opener at home to the Washington Huskies Saturday afternoon, 33-14. A junior tailback named Clarence McDaniel had waltzed through the Bruin defense for 141 yards and three touchdowns.

"You want to know how I'm doing," Gunner said.

Del looked up from the business section of the paper and set it aside, for good. "Yeah, I would," he said, signaling their waitress for more coffee.

Del Curry was a good looking little man in his early

forties who was hard to lie to, face-to-face. His skin was light brown and his full head of hair was an almost golden yellow. He had a well-groomed mustache and the eyes of a stuffed bird on a taxidermist's shelf, black and unwavering gems of glass.

"I'm doing fine," Gunner said, plastering a slice of white toast with grape jelly.

"Yeah?"

"Yeah."

"You get your money up front like I told you?"

"I got enough to work with."

"And the rest?"

"The rest comes later. When I'm done."

"Uh-huh."

"It's working out this time, Del. Really." He braved a short glance Del's way. "It's not the same worthless shit as before."

Del's gaze was unyielding. "This is *different* worthless shit," he said.

Gunner just lowered his head and resumed eating.

The bulletin board at the converted corner market the Brothers of Volition called home was uninspiring reading, but it was all the diversion the barren anteroom offered to visitors killing time there.

Posted on the board's cork face were bits and pieces of the propaganda upon which the Brothers based their sometimes contradictory socialist/black nationalist code: photocopied newspaper clippings from various left-wing periodicals, excerpts from the writings of Karl Marx and Malcolm X, and a colorful collection of inflammatory quotations made by white Americans of considerable political influence, from members of the L.A. School Board to Secretaries of State, both past and present. A hand-lettered banner at the top of the board read, in wavering capitals, WAKE UP, BROTHERS AND SISTERS! WAKE UP!

Gunner gave the board one final, lingering look and

took a seat on one of the hard plastic chairs arranged beside it. Not far away, the round-faced kid with the outdated, balloon-like Afro whose job it was to watch the door was still taking him in, glassy-eyed, propped up behind a painted metal desk like a mannequin with an attitude problem. Decked out in the Brothers' standard uniform of green dungaree shirt and blue denim pants, he had assured Gunner that the detective was welcome to wait around for Brother Mayes to return from the Black Student Union rally he was addressing on the campus of Cal State Long Beach, but he had neglected to mention how severely Gunner would be scrutinized if he chose to do so. Working for Verna Gail may have earned him the right to cool his heels on the premises until Mayes could dismiss him personally, but it obviously didn't make him a friend of the family.

Gunner spent the next two hours under the microscope of the kid's undivided attention, melting in the sweltering heat of the room, and was back up at the bulletin board, about to call it quits, when Mayes and his requisite tour party of a half-dozen or so compatriots finally made their entrance.

Wearing the Brothers' colors to a man, they were in good spirits, chatting among themselves like a band of GI's returning from battle. One, a lean, pale-skinned man in his early thirties, was training a VCR camcorder on the others, recording the moment for posterity.

Gunner went unnoticed until his friend at the door pulled Mayes aside to point him out, making a brief, indiscernible comment as he did so. Mayes came forward and Gunner let him, as seven pairs of eyes looked him over like an unmarked parcel making ticking sounds on their doorstep.

"So you're Gunner. Verna's private cop." Mayes appraised him with open amusement, chuckling briefly, expending little energy. "Something told me I'd be hearing from you, sooner or later."

He was a smooth, heavy man with muscles, dark-skinned and imposing. His hair cut down to a mere shadow on his scalp, he had large, almond-shaped eyes and an impeccable complexion, and his handshake was firm, unyielding. Gunner had read somewhere that he was closing in on forty, but he didn't look it; there was a vibrancy about him that seldom reared its head beyond a man's early twenties.

He had been followed over to Gunner's side of the room by a short, spindly block of granite with a stone wall's disposition, a cool little youngblood whose clothes fit his body like a thin coat of paint, and he watched Gunner square off with Mayes the way guards at the Louvre watch patrons admire the Mona Lisa.

"Mouse" was a damn good name for him.

"I'm predictable like that," Gunner said, his eyes on Mouse. "Seems like something's always telling somebody where I'm going, or what I'm about to do next. Sometimes even why."

"'Why' is a given. You're a cop. And cops pick brains. You're here to pick mine."

Mayes smiled. Gunner wasn't fond of his choice of words, but was disinclined to mention it. "If you want to look at it that way," he said.

"I'd rather not look at it at all, you want to know the truth. It's been a long day." Mayes looked over his shoulder at Mouse. "Hasn't it, Brother M.?"

Mouse kept his eyes on Gunner and nodded, his tiny head moving obliquely.

Mayes grinned and turned around again. "Forgive my manners. This is Brother Stokes, our captain of the guard. Some of the Brothers have been known to call him Mouse on occasion, but not to his face. Never to his face. He's a sensitive man, Brother M."

"I'll only need five minutes," Gunner said, getting edgy.

Mayes stopped smiling. "I'm sorry, Cop. But I'm afraid I can't see where talking to you would accomplish anything. In fact, I doubt it ever does." He turned away to leave.

Gunner grabbed him just above the right elbow and spun him around, glowering. *"Five minutes,* Mayes," he said, drawing Mayes to him, as Mouse and the others converged upon him in a concerted swarm.

The largest two Brothers in the group, the bouquet-headed kid at the door and another, leaner man, took him from behind, pulling him away from Mayes, and secured his arms, holding him for Mouse. As Mayes stepped clear, Mouse closed in, but not fast enough: Gunner broke his right hand loose and jarred the little man with it, hammering Mouse's cheekbone just below the left eye. The doorman's friend to Gunner's right drove a fist like a jackhammer into the investigator's rib cage once, twice, and doubled him up, giving Mouse a moment to recover. In short order Mouse retaliated with an overhand left, then straightened the detective up again with a knee under Gunner's chin.

He tried to follow with a looping overhand right, but Mayes stepped in to intercede.

"The man obviously takes his work more seriously than I," he said, watching Gunner crumple to the floor as the giants behind him released him. "He's deluded. Not dangerous."

On his knees, Gunner held his insides in place with an open hand and raised his head, licking blood and perspiration from one corner of his mouth. The Brother with the VCR camcorder was still rolling tape, aiming the instrument's large convex eye squarely on him, crouching from a short distance for an intimate close-up. Mayes was now as solemn as Mouse, apparently unfazed by this latest of small victories for his Brothers of Volition.

"Let's go, Cop," he said, gesturing for his guest to get up off the floor. "If you can make it back to my office, I'll give you a few minutes of my time. To enlighten you, if you will."

He walked away, toward the rear of the building. Gunner pushed himself to his feet and followed, slowly, braving the tense gauntlet of the doorman and company, trailing Mouse and the Brothers' resident cameraman behind him. He moved into the gutted bowels of the failed corner market past identically dressed Brothers of all ages feeding paper to an antiquated printing press and pounding manual typewriters, talking on telephones and painting various placards. The building was a mess, a patched and repatched three-alarm fire hazard, but the floors were clean and the rooms well illuminated, some fresh with the scent of ammonia and disinfectant.

Mayes himself had a small office in a rear corner, not far from the large bay door that had been the former market's delivery entrance. The room was big enough to hold a desk, three wooden chairs, and a filing cabinet, but little else. A transistor radio sat atop the filing cabinet and a calendar was nailed to one wall. Sharing the surface of the desk with a meticulous arrangement of paperwork was an IBM PC and an electric fan that was only moving hot air more rapidly through the room. A good-sized observation window near the door gave Mayes an unobstructed view of his soldiers at work, hammering, typing, painting away like Santa's little helpers.

Mayes took his seat behind the desk and waved Gunner into one of the remaining two chairs before him. The detective chose the one to Mayes's right, farthest from the door, and Mouse grabbed the other, dragging it to the back of the room before sitting down, so that he might observe Gunner without being easily observed himself.

Gunner glanced at him back there, amused, and started to join him, just to get a reaction, but turned around to face Mayes instead. He had an idea the time would come soon enough to have more fun with Mouse.

"Brother Jamaal doesn't bother you?" Mayes asked Gunner, referring to the Brother now setting the VCR camcorder up on a tripod at the room's open door.

"Not unless you're going to ask me to strip," Gunner said, hurting. He was trying to find a comfortable position in his chair. "That something you do for everybody you ask back here? Or just the most photogenic?"

"It's merely a toy I like to play with. My way of avoiding any confusion as to what has or has not been said here, by whom and in what context." Mayes smiled. "Can I get you anything to drink? A beer, some wine—a bottle of carbonated bourgeois water, perhaps?"

Gunner shook his head. "No thanks."

"We can send Brother M. out, if there's something you'd like in particular."

Gunner paused, looked back at Mouse indifferently, then regarded Mayes again. "How about a Red Rooster Ale?"

Mouse stood up, anticipating the order to leave.

To Gunner, Mayes said, "Red Rooster Ale's an Australian brew. Very big in Johannesburg, I believe."

"Yeah?"

"They don't export it to the States, however. Unless you know something I don't."

Gunner didn't. "Is that a problem?"

Mouse sat down again.

Mayes checked to see that Brother Jamaal was again rolling tape. "What do you want, Gunner?" he asked, impolitely.

"I want to know who killed Denny Townsend," Gunner said, succinctly.

Mayes didn't flinch. "Who's Denny Townsend?"

"You need a hint?"

"Please."

"He was bigger than a breadbox," Gunner said. "And *white*."

Mayes still didn't flinch, but this time a certain amount of effort seemed to be involved. "You're referring to the man you were looking for for Verna."

"The pale fellow with the scattergun left eye, yeah. Don't tell me you didn't know?"

Mayes shrugged. "*I* wasn't looking for him. Why should I know?"

Gunner answered one shrug with another. "Because you would have wanted to," he said. "And with more people in the field than UPI, you had the means to get word before the body was cold."

"Except I didn't get any word."

He was looking past Gunner at Mouse, an accusatory glint in his eye. "You're the first to give the white boy a name. You say it was Townsend?"

"Townsend, right. First name Denny. You want the proper spelling, go down to the morgue and read the tag he'll have hanging off one of his toes." Gunner stopped, squinting, and waited for a sharp, sudden pain to subside along his right lower torso. The simple task of breathing was beginning to entail substantial discomfort. "It won't tell you how he got there, of course, but then, neither will anyone else. Because nobody seems to know. Or cares to say."

"Including you?"

"What I know about it isn't worth repeating, but it doesn't take long to recite, so I'll bore you with it. Sometime last Thursday someone put a bullet in his liver just north of the family jewels and left him in a conspicuous place to die. The idea, I think, was to make it look as if I'd done it on Verna's behalf."

"But you didn't, of course."

"No. Which should explain why I'm here, bothering a busy man like you."

He was watching Mayes's eyes for signs of disruption, seeing little in them but momentary flashes of reflected light. Mouse was making restless noises from his chair at the back of the room.

With some indignation, Mayes said, "We didn't kill that white boy, Gunner. Use your head."

Gunner said nothing.

"Hell," Mayes said, "who needed him dead? He was a powerful tool for the cause, alive and kicking. It made him easier to hate. Another champion of white American justice, unpunished and unrepentant, free to kill again."

"Come on, Brother Mayes. Save it. That rationale sounded lame when Verna first quoted you, and it sounds just as lame now. Townsend didn't send the Brothers an obscene telegram, he murdered Buddy Dorris—the second most influential figure in your organization and, some say, its lifeblood. You wanted him dead, all right. To say otherwise is to insult my intelligence."

Mayes seemed undecided as to how to react to being called, in essence, a liar. "The prospect of avenging Buddy's murder intrigued me, of course. As it has a great many Brothers, I'm sure. Buddy was, as you say, a primary factor in our success to this point. But what the Brothers do they do by decree, and the Brothers did not call, officially or otherwise, for Townsend's assassination. He'd have been dead weeks ago if we had."

"Maybe one of your boys didn't feel like he needed to call a vote on it. Surely they don't all walk the party line infallibly?"

"If that concept gives you trouble, you have my apology, but that happens to be the case with the Brothers of Volition. We're a unified front. Individuals working as a whole, for the whole. We don't go in for any of that aimless, disorganized free-lance shit the Panthers tried twenty years ago."

"The way I remember it, they didn't exactly plan to be disorganized. It just sort of worked out that way. A dumb recruit here, and a dumb recruit there . . ."

"We don't *have* any dumb recruits," Mayes said. "This isn't some halfway house for every black man, woman, or child armed with a grudge against Whitey. This is an association of *winners*. People with vision and foresight."

He was wearing his game face now, setting his forced

hospitality aside, at least for the moment. "No bloodsuckers," he said, leaning forward on his desk, closing the distance between himself and Gunner strategically. "No parasites. None of the spineless opportunists who feed upon the weak among us with one scam after another, thinking themselves adept at what the Man likes to call 'free enterprise.'"

"You mean scumbags like me," Gunner said.

Mayes grinned. "Unless I've misjudged you. Verna's been paying you what, forty-five dollars a day, plus expenses?"

"Are you asking as the lady's friend, or as her financial consultant?"

"What's the difference?"

"The difference is, if you're asking as her financial consultant, you can go fuck yourself."

"And if I'm asking as her friend? As someone who doesn't care to see Buddy's sister get the short end of a stick?"

"In that case, you can get fucked. That's not a big difference, I know. But it's something."

Mouse was moving behind him. Gunner started to turn, braced to leave his chair, but Mayes chopped the air with an open hand to wave the young man off, back to his seat in the distance.

"Forget it," he said, glaring at Gunner. "The man wants to be unreceptive, that's his privilege."

Gunner watched Mouse sit down again and grinned. The skin beneath the Brother's left eye was pink and shiny, stretched across his cheekbone over swollen flesh.

Mouse had a mouse.

Gunner said to Mayes, "You toss him the Milk Bone now, or later?"

"Save the hard-boiled shtick for your morning shave, Cop. You're funny enough without it. Private Dick Gunner, heavy on the case."

"That's me."

"You have any more questions, Dick, or am I free to go now?"

"The way it works, I don't ask any more questions until I get an answer to my first one."

"Shit. I answered it. I'll answer it again. The Brothers don't give a damn that your white boy's dead, and we don't give a damn how he got that way. His death changes nothing, just as I told Verna it would. Buddy's still gone and we're no closer now to the world we seek to build than we were to begin with."

"For a man who was supposed to be Buddy's brother—without the capital *b*—your pragmatism is amazing."

"So I'm pragmatic. What of it? Does my being pragmatic mean I don't miss the man? Like I'd miss my right hand, or an arm, or a leg if I were to lose any one of those just as suddenly?

"I'd love to raise holy hell over my fallen comrade, I assure you, but I have a revolution to lead. I have responsibilities. And I can't afford to get caught up in an overemotional trip that could destroy my focus and set the Brothers back beyond any feasible point of recovery.

"Time marches on, Gunner. Sociopolitical congregations evolve or disintegrate. To survive, we've no choice but to begin anew, to lay Buddy to rest and get on with the next phase of our existence. And the sooner we do, the better. For everyone."

His sudden cool was a natural act, uncontrived and effortless. There was no emotion being suppressed here, no passion taking cover behind a false veil of calm—this was the real thing.

Apathy to the tenth degree.

"I can't help wondering if Buddy would have been as quick to dismiss your legacy had Townsend come looking for you and not him," Gunner said.

Mouse laughed behind him, holding the question in low esteem, and Mayes peered around Gunner to grin at him, sharing the gag. To Gunner, he said, "I think it would be safe to say that Buddy would have taken my loss somewhat harder than I have taken his. At least on the surface."

"A little harder, yeah," Mouse said, breaking his self-imposed silence at last. His was the voice of a much larger man, low and short of breath, and now Gunner understood why he so rarely used it. It was as poor a match for his modest build as any voice could have possibly been.

Mayes seemed as surprised to hear him speak as Gunner. He looked at the bony young man like a toy the detective had broken that would never work quite right again. "What he would have done, Gunner, my man, is go *berserk,*" he said finally, distracted. "Off. Strap a harpoon to the hood of his car and lead the troops to battle. Not for me, specifically, you understand. But for the *Brothers.* Any Brother. Townsend could've had his pick."

At the back of the room, Mouse was nodding his head vigorously, laughing his big man's laugh again.

"You didn't know him," Mayes said, sharing yet another fraternal grin with his first lieutenant. "You can't imagine the damage he would have done, given the chance. Verna can tell you. Buddy had been ready for his emancipation since the age of eight, was tired of waiting for it and sick of pleading for it, and had made up his mind he was going to live to see it, one way or another, even if he had to tow the rest of us shiftless black folk along for the ride."

"And yet he was never the Brother of mention," Gunner noted. "You were."

"Yes. Naturally. I was the Brother who knew how to spell *cat* without a *k.*"

Mouse thought that, too, was funny, but this time his laughter was short-lived.

"Then why kill *him*?" Gunner asked, bluntly. "Why kill Buddy, and not you?"

It was a fair enough question, one a blind man would have asked eventually, but that didn't seem to help Mayes answer it. He stared at Gunner blankly, with what looked like legitimate bewilderment, and shook his head. "I don't know," he said. "I've wondered about that myself. Buddy was a more accessible target than I, certainly. And I suppose some could have seen his general lack of predictability as a more threatening trait than my intellect and/or communicative skills."

"But if the intention was to strike a killing blow to your movement," Gunner said, "you were still the obvious choice. Not Buddy."

"Yes."

"And yet Townsend went after him."

Mayes shrugged, noncommittally. "So you say."

Gunner had a sudden thought, a buried jewel of the subconscious that chose this moment to come to light. Another late arrival of the obvious. "Could it be that Buddy's murder had nothing to do with the Brothers? That it was something other than politically motivated?"

Mayes shrugged again, trying to come off as bored. "Anything's possible," he said. "But a white man would've been hard pressed to hold a *personal* grudge against Buddy, considering Buddy never associated with one long enough to offend him."

"Maybe it wasn't a white man he offended," Gunner said, impulsively.

Mayes laughed. Mouse, strangely, didn't follow his lead. "You've got to be joking. Buddy's friends at the Deuce—Gaines the custodian and Sheila the whore—may be a little dense, and generally drunk as hell to boot, but I think they know a white man when they see one. Don't you?"

"You're talking about the gunman. I'm talking about the man—or men—who may have paid him."

Mayes did another fine impression of a stone. "Who said anybody did?"

Gunner's eyes had shifted from Mayes to the calendar hanging on the wall to his left, just above his head. It was an advertising tool for a local mortuary, cheap and poorly illustrated, featuring capsulized biographies of notable black Americans throughout history. October was Nat Turner month. A man with the same goals as Mayes claimed to have today, as Dorris had had only weeks ago: to free the slaves. Get out from under the white man's thumb and multiply, prosper.

Maybe Mayes and Dorris would each have an October to call their own, someday.

Gunner looked at Mayes again. "Townsend paid a bag man good money to make a drop of some personal items just hours before he died. The kind of money a one-eyed man doesn't make selling magazine subscriptions door to door."

"How do you know?"

"I saw the exchange. Or part of it."

Mayes's eyes left Gunner's to glance at Mouse for a nearly indiscernible instant. "What did this bag man look like?"

Gunner shook his head, smiling. "Give me more credit than that, Mayes. Shit."

"I was only about to propose that we talk to him. Civilly. What you did with him afterward would be your business."

"I think I know my business, thanks."

"You think you can find him alone?"

"I never said I intended to try."

"You have something better to do?"

"I don't know. Something else could turn up. Tomorrow's a new day."

Gunner dragged a hand across his forehead, perspiring profusely. The heat in the room was stifling, undaunted by the efforts of the overmatched fan to diminish it, and his clothes were glued to his skin.

"You're making things unnecessarily hard on yourself," Mayes said, shrugging. "You'd like to know who killed Townsend, and we'd like to know who, if anyone, he was working for when he murdered Buddy. *If* he murdered Buddy. A fool with a gun is one thing; a conspiracy's something else. It'd save us both a lot of time if we could look for your bag man together."

Gunner shook his head again. "I'm afraid that wouldn't work out, Brother Mayes," he said, standing up to leave.

Mayes remained seated, smiling minimally. "No? And why is that?"

Gunner directed his answer at Mouse, ignoring Mayes completely. "Because I only make an ass out of myself once a month," he said. "And the next Brother I catch in my peripheral vision, I'm going to cripple. Whether they seem to be following me or not."

He gave Mouse a good half-minute to absorb the threat, then saluted Mayes with a little nod and went to the door, aching, confronting the camcorder barring his way there directly. Brother Jamaal looked up from its eyepiece and stepped aside for him, his face bearing no suggestion of malice. When Gunner kicked the tripod out from under the camcorder as he passed it, sending the tape machine crashing to the hard concrete floor, Brother Jamaal's face looked quite different.

"Special effects," Gunner said to him, before strolling casually out the way he'd come in.

8

ichael "Brush" Bush wouldn't invite Gunner into his home, or join him out on the front porch. He couldn't have been more inhospitable if Gunner had been a perfect stranger trying to unload encyclopedias; he just stood there on the other side of his front door, holding it open only marginally, and shook his top-heavy head from side to side, disturbing not a strand of the kinky black hair pointed skyward on top of it.

"No can do, 'Ron. Sorry."

Gunner upped the ante of his bribe to an even fifty, baiting Brush with the sight of yet another twenty-dollar bill. "Gimme a break, Brush," he said wearily.

"It ain't the money, man. I'd do it for nothin' if I could, but I can't. I shouldn't'a done it the last time, you wanna know the truth."

Brush was a thirty-one-year-old Senior Clerk for the California Department of Motor Vehicles Gunner had once shadowed for three weeks at the behest of a jealous wife.

Most jealous wives would have been relieved to hear that Gunner had found Brush to be nothing if not a monogamous, happily married man, but it happened that Gunner's client was someone else's jealous wife, not Brush's, and so the news had a somewhat atypical affect on the lady. In all likelihood, she would have succeeded in parting her old flame's hair with a carving knife had Gunner not made the unethical decision to warn Brush she might be coming, and Gunner had been exploiting the man's gratitude ever since.

"All I need is a name and an address, Brush. It's an easy fifty bucks, man."

Brush shook his head again. From the neck up, he *did* look like a Fuller brush. "They watchin' the database like a hawk, 'Ron. They catch me at a terminal lookin' up shit for you, I'm dead. You gonna take care of my family while I look for another job? Huh?"

"Then just get me a name. I'll get the address myself."

"Forget it, man. I told you. No can do. Sorry."

He closed the door without saying good-bye. Gunner stood on the porch for a moment, staring the door to the little house down, before putting his fifty dollars back in his pocket and retreating, thinking, hoping that maybe the fat man in the retired Postal Service jeep wasn't worth talking to, anyway.

Favoring his tender ribs, Gunner lowered himself gingerly into the Cobra and checked his watch. It was a good twenty minutes after six. The street lamps in Carson were already glowing and all the kids in Brush's neighborhood had been reeled in for the night. So much for Gunner's Sunday. Better luck Monday.

However the hell he was going to spend it.

Late the next morning, Gunner slapped two slices of white toast around a hard fried egg and, still chasing the tandem down with a cup of strong coffee, caught up with Mean Sheila as she made her renewed rounds of the newly redeveloped storefronts along Compton Boulevard just east of Santa Fe, back in the hunt now that Denny Townsend was safely out of her hair. Word of the white boy's death had not yet been made public, but Gunner understood that Sheila had news sources of her own, fast and reliable. He asked her how Muhammad Ali was doing, referring to Ray Hollins with all due respect, and she told him with no noticeable sense of loss that Hollins was back in Motown, had been since last Friday despite the police department's recommendation that he remain in California until further notice. Sheila said he had been with her all of Thursday afternoon, and somehow Gunner believed her enough to leave it at that. His questions didn't seem to bother her anymore so it figured there weren't any recent murder conspiracies in her past.

Having convinced himself all over again that time spent with Sheila was time poorly spent, Gunner was finally left with but a single "lead" to pursue, if one chose to use the term loosely. From a pay phone not far from Sheila's hunting grounds, he silenced the prerecorded voice of an operator with forty-five cents in change and dialed the number someone had scrawled on the back of the "Henshaw for Congress" flyer he had lifted from Denny Townsend's apartment four days ago. The line rang in his ear a long ten seconds before a cheery female voice said, "Henshaw's the Right Man, Larry Stewart's desk," disdaining any form of hello altogether.

It seemed Gunner had called Henshaw's west L.A. campaign headquarters in Brentwood. That in itself wasn't too surprising—Henshaw would have been the "right man" for Townsend, to be sure—but the particular phone Gunner had set to ringing there was.

Because Larry Stewart was no volunteer flunky screening calls at Henshaw's base of operations between tours of duty at the Xerox machine, but was, in fact, the would-be Congressman's campaign manager. The kind of upper-echelon cog in the candidate's political machine who could be expected to take calls on his private line from Oscar-winning actors and famous labor leaders, magazine editors and political pollsters and forecasters—but not from psychotic, uneducated low-lifes like Denny Townsend.

And yet Townsend had somehow come upon Stewart's phone number.

A minor enigma, perhaps, but Gunner decided to explore it just the same, having little else to do with his time. If all Townsend had been was one man with a plan, just another nut looking to get his name read aloud on the evening news, then Gunner had already seen the people who would have most wanted him dead, and there wasn't much left for him to do except wait around for one of them to make a mistake. But if, by chance, Townsend had been something more—like a front man for one or more crazies of his demented persuasion, as his generosity toward his fat friend in the windbreaker seemed to suggest—then it was possible his death had come at the hands of people Gunner had not yet been introduced to, but would have to acquaint himself with soon.

Very soon.

So he told one big Black Lie over the phone and got himself in the door of Lewis Henshaw's campaign headquarters on Wilshire and Yale, where Brentwood and Santa Monica came effortlessly together. A failed auto parts store had been stripped to its bare walls to make room for a small army of Henshaw's faithful and enough second-hand furniture and ringing telephones to keep them feeling relatively at home. They were a diverse group, Henshaw's people—short and white, tall and white, fat and white. It appeared the forty-six-year-old Chicago cop-turned-novelist/film consultant/politician was still unwilling to concede that the white vote alone was not going to get him over in the multi-ethnic wonderland that was west Los Angeles.

And that was just as well, Gunner mused, as he integrated the aspiring Congressman's camp with his arrival, because with Henshaw's record as a pig-headed, prejudicial applicator of the law in Illinois, the white vote was all he was likely to get, whether he liked it or not.

"Where would I find Larry Stewart?" Gunner asked a young man filling a paper cup at the water cooler near the door. The face that turned his way looked like an acne sampler, red and roughly textured.

The man caught his cup before it could hit the floor, closed his slack jaw, and pointed to a pair of half-height glass and fiberboard partitions arranged around one corner of the floor space in the rear.

For an executive of Stewart's stature, it wasn't much of an office, but the cold young beauty manning his desk inside seemed to take the responsibility of guarding it for him quite seriously.

"You didn't sound black over the phone," she said, her eyes taking Gunner in with open skepticism, not the least bit afraid to insult him. The solid gray business suit she wore didn't have a crease in it, and she did as much for it as it did for her.

Gunner smiled agreeably and sat down.

"So I've been told," he said. "Must be all those big words I use. Like *who, what,* and *where.*"

She either didn't understand him, or didn't particularly care to. Without changing expression she introduced herself as someone named Terry Allison, Larry Stewart's personal secretary and chief liaison with the volunteers under his command, and she was far more attractive than her voice, transmitted over an ambiance-filled telephone line, could have possibly made clear. She was an intoxicating distillation of southern California Dreamgirl prerequisites, a cliché come to life: moist blue eyes offset by skin the color of bronze, tanned to perfection and glowing; sandy blond hair giving off light like the sun, cut with a surgeon's eye to the precise length of her shoulders.

And people liked to say they had been drawn to California by the weather.

"Larry's in San Francisco," she said when she was

good and ready, and not a moment before. "With Lew. I'm afraid he won't be back in Los Angeles until Thursday morning sometime."

She meant Gunner to take the news as a dismissal; she put a *Don't Call Us, We'll Call You* smile on her face and fell silent.

"He been there long?" Gunner asked, pretending to miss her point entirely.

"Since Friday evening. Lew was a guest speaker at the Bay Area Veterans' Association conference over the weekend, and asked Larry to tag along. Why?"

Gunner shrugged. "Just curious."

"Exactly what kind of story is it you're writing, Mr. . . . ."

"Gunner."

"That's right. Mr. Gunner. What's the slant of your piece, Mr. Gunner? What's the angle?"

"Angle?"

"The angle, yes. You do know what an angle is, don't you?"

"Oh, yeah. Sure. What's a newspaper story without an angle?"

"I thought you said you were with *Newsweek*. The magazine."

Gunner shrugged again. "I don't recall exactly what I said, frankly. *Newsweek* or the *Daily News,* one or the other. Does it matter?"

Her eyes left him for a moment, perhaps searching the crowded floor beyond Stewart's quarters for a worker ant big enough to bounce Gunner out on his ear. He had made quite a stir out there among them earlier, as totally out of place as he was, and the novelty of his presence had not worn off yet. With the attention he was continuing to draw, help was just a raised voice away if the lady decided to ask for it.

"You're not a reporter, then?"

"No." Gunner dropped his wallet on Stewart's desk

where she could see it, open to his license in its yellowing plastic window. She read it right down to the fine print on the back, and more than once.

"You're a private detective," she said, pushing the wallet back across the desk at him, making the job sound like something she came across every day. It was beginning to look as if nothing Gunner had to offer was going to particularly move her one way or the other. "And you want to see Larry because . . . ?"

"Because I'm in deep shit," Gunner said, letting some of his irritation with her condescending manner show through, "and his phone number was burning a hole in my pocket. I found it among the personal effects of a friend of his and I was hoping he could tell me how it got there."

"A friend of Larry's?" More blatant skepticism. "Who?"

"His name was Denny Townsend. He was a white man, medium height, in his early thirties. Had a psyche only a mother could love and a left eye with more moves than a good game of chess. Sound familiar?"

Her face said it did, losing its well-defined implacability all at once. Gunner suddenly had her full attention, if not her total respect. "We have a worker," she said, choosing her words carefully. "A volunteer, who comes in now and then to run errands for the staff. He's not on our regular rolls, so I can't look it up, but his name *could* be Denny. And I suppose he does have an eye similar to what you describe." She was trying to remember him in detail, creating a stubborn silence. "You say he had Larry's private number? The one you used earlier?"

Gunner nodded and showed her the flyer, without actually handing it to her. "These errands you say he ran. He run many of them for Stewart personally?"

She shook her head. "No. I don't think so."

"But this is Stewart's handwriting?"

She gave the flyer a second, closer look. "It could be. But I don't see how. If the man you're referring to is the one I have in mind, Larry could not have intended this for him. Because Larry's had no use for this fellow; he's unfit for most things. In fact . . ."

She didn't go on.

Gunner waited.

Allison shrugged and said, "I was just going to say that it wouldn't really surprise me if your being here has something to do with his landing in some kind of trouble with the law. He's that type, I think."

"Yeah?"

She nodded. "I haven't had much contact with him myself, actually, but what I've had sort of leads me to believe he could be dangerous to some people, under the wrong circumstances. Exactly what kind of trouble is he in?"

Gunner smiled wryly. "The worst possible. Somebody caught *him* 'under the wrong circumstances' and put a hole in his pelvic region too big to sew up. He's dead."

Stewart's phone rang abruptly. Allison seemed too preoccupied to answer it at first, but picked it up on the third ring and made short work of the call, slightly flustered and embarrassed to be so. When she turned to Gunner again, she had the look of someone who had lost her place in time and needed some help getting resynchronized with the universe.

"He was murdered," Gunner said simply, anxious to move along. "Two and a half weeks after knocking off Buddy Dorris of the Brothers of Volition and a bartender too slow to stop him."

Allison sat up in her chair. If she wasn't genuinely surprised, she had some talent for pretending to be.

"How's that again?"

"Buddy Dorris. Your boy Townsend was the hero who put the hit on him. You did know Buddy Dorris?"

"Of course."

"But you weren't aware that Townsend had killed him?"

Her contempt for the question was such that she declined to answer it.

"What do you want, Mr. Gunner? Spell it out, please."

Gunner eagerly complied. "I want to talk to Stewart," he said. "I want to ask him where Townsend got the idea to blow Dorris's head off, and whether he got it before Stewart gave him his number, or after. What do you think?"

"I think you've made a big mistake, that's what I think. I think you're looking for the wrong man."

"Meaning who? Townsend or Stewart?"

"Take your pick. I don't believe our man killed anybody, in the first place. And in the second, I'm certain no one here knew anything about it if he did. Larry most especially."

She was back in the saddle again, chin held high and proud. Gunner glared at her renewed infuriating smugness and said, "Somebody somewhere did."

"Really."

"Yeah. Really. Townsend didn't have the brainpower to tie his shoes without help, even you'd have to admit that. So he sure as hell didn't do such a smash-up job taking Dorris out working all by his lonesome. He got assistance. Direction. Probably from the same party or parties trying to frame a good friend of mine for his murder."

"And you think Larry is involved somehow?"

"I've never met Larry. You tell me. Why would a man in his position lay his private number on a fruitcake like Denny Townsend? Just to have his own certified psycho fetch his lunch from time to time?"

"I'm sure his reasons were more substantial than that," Allison said, "but exactly what they were, I wouldn't know. *I* certainly never considered using him for anything."

"But if he had been working under Stewart for the campaign, performing legitimate duties of some kind, you'd have known about it?"

Allison shrugged. "In most cases, yes. Generally, Larry and I run this office together, in tandem, but we occasionally run our own little projects on the side. Is that a crime?"

Gunner shook his head. "Not unless Stewart's idea of a little project is vastly different from mine."

"Then you won't be needing to talk to him after all. Will you?"

She was trying to nudge the black man out the door again. Either she didn't care for the nature of his business, or she was very uncomfortable around people more darkly tanned than she. Exactly which of the two was the case, Gunner couldn't say.

"If it's all the same to you," he said, firmly and with no great emotion, mastering his ebbing patience well, "I'd prefer to, regardless."

"He'll only repeat what I've already told you."

"Somehow, I don't doubt that. But I have to give it a shot just the same. He may not be up to admitting guilt of any kind, but he just might give me some insight into the way Townsend's mind worked. Who the man's friends were and where they hung out. Maybe even what they planned to do about the nationwide *nigger problem* your man Henshaw's so concerned about."

The liquid blue eyes lost their gleam. He had finally said something the blond could not deflect with moderate ease. "Lew Henshaw is not that kind of man," she said angrily.

Gunner had to laugh. "How do you mean that, exactly? That he's not the kind of man who likes to think of us black folk in those terms? Or rather that he's never been dumb enough to publicly refer to us quite so disparagingly?"

"I mean that he's not the racist, red-necked anachronism the press makes him out to be. Lew is a good man, Mr. Gunner. A fair man. And he doesn't think of you people—of anyone—in that way."

There. She had clarified it. Gunner *was* one of *Them*.
A colored boy by any other name . . .

He wanted to laugh again, but found that he could not.
Stupidity and raw beauty, especially in one so young, was
no laughable mix. "You think he's just talking about law
and order, I guess. All that shit about 'returning the streets
to our children,' and 'raising justice from the dead.'"

"Lew wants an America we can all be proud of. All of
us. You see something sinister in that?"

"He's looking for *war*, lady. Not justice or freedom or
any of those other flag-waving catch phrases his kind likes
to throw around. He's looking for war, in the streets. Between the white hats and the black hats, the good guys and
the bad. You and me, Ms. Allison. One-on-one."

The blond shook her head at him, the way she probably had at her mother as a little girl. "You're wrong. You
don't know Lew. That isn't what he wants at all."

She had lost a step somewhere, and the difference in
her countenance was startling. She had taken up Henshaw's
defense before, Gunner realized, to fend off other argu-
ments along the same vein, other foes with similar angles of
attack, and the wear and tear on her convictions was beginning to show through. It was a difficult business, obviously,
believing in the dormant goodness of a basically parasitic
man.

She got to her feet behind Stewart's desk and gave
Gunner one more glimpse of the armor-clad exterior she
had shown before. School was out.

"If you have no more questions for me, Mr. Gunner,
you'll excuse me. But I'm afraid I have better things to do
with my time than lobby for a vote Lew is clearly not going
to get, no matter what kind of man he may or may not be.
If you'll leave me your card, I'll be sure to see that Larry
gets back to you as soon as he possibly can."

Gunner took her in from where he sat and made a
long, drawn-out exercise of pulling a business card from his
wallet, teeming with ambivalence. The woman was young

and well educated, easy on the eye and full of good intentions, but what she knew about black people wouldn't make a short paragraph, and there was a sadness in that he could not reconcile.

He flipped his card in her general direction and stood up.

"Thanks for the time," he said, and left her before the impulse to slap his third woman in six days grew too strong to overcome.

Outside, Gunner reached his car and came to notice a familiar vehicle pulling up to the curb nearby.

An old Postal Service jeep, badly painted and dented on one side.

Its driver, a giant man with a meager mustache, heaved a heavy box of what looked like computer paper from the jeep's passenger seat and took it inside Henshaw's campaign quarters. He hadn't recognized Gunner.

But Gunner had recognized him, yellow windbreaker or no.

enny Townsend's fat errand boy worked some long hours for Lewis Henshaw. The California skyline was tying up the loose ends of a fast fade to black, well after 6 P.M., when he finally called it a day and drove home to a little one-bedroom house with wood slat sides and a tar-paper roof on the seedier side of Venice, far removed from the Pacific Ocean and its neighboring affluent real estate. Situated near the east end of the 12000 block of Victoria Avenue, the house was an architectural corpse, weather-beaten and lifeless. No lights shone in the windows; no sounds crept through the walls.

Townsend's friend had to open the gate of a chain-link fence surrounding the property to pull his jeep into the driveway. When he went back to lock it behind him, Gunner was standing there waiting, the only living soul on the street. The black man offered him an extended peek at the heavy S&W .357 in his right-hand coat pocket, giving him time to study its form in the dark, then stepped quickly inside the gate to join him on the other side of the fence.

"You want to live to see another Hostess Twinkie, open the front door and keep your mouth shut," Gunner said, nodding toward the house.

The big man gave every indication that he was about to lose his lunch—his face had turned the unsettling shade of an August moon and his skin was lightly dotted with a cold sweat—but he managed to do as he was told without much deviation. He produced his keys at the door, entered the house with Gunner close behind, and waited for further instructions as the black man found a light switch with his free hand.

Gunner glanced around and grimaced. The living room was right out of a Grandmothers' Surplus catalog: cheap Indian throw rugs and bland-colored draperies, porcelain knickknacks in waist-high showcases and unreadable books killing time on dusty shelves. An old console TV stood at center ring, squaring off with an oversized sofa as a listless brass floor lamp played referee.

The east wing of the Playboy Mansion, it wasn't.

"What do you want?" the big man asked, finding the nerve to distance himself from Gunner by a good eight feet. His color had not improved.

"Your wallet," Gunner said, now wielding the .357 openly, leaving no doubt as to where it was aimed. "For starters. Slide it over across the floor. Easy."

Again, the big man cooperated.

Gunner found the driver's license at the front of the wallet and looked it over, keeping one wary eye on its owner.

"Says here your name is Stanley Ferris. That your real name, Ferris, or just something you made up?"

Ferris swallowed hard and said, "It's my name."

"Your friends call you Stan, I guess."

Ferris nodded.

III

Gunner tossed the big man's wallet back to him and, with some amazement, said, "You don't remember me, do you, Stan?"

Ferris didn't, obviously, until Gunner pantomimed opening his fly with his free hand, the way he had in the locker room at the Hollywood YMCA.

"Oh, Christ," the big man said, his knees starting to buckle.

"You going to faint?"

"I think so. Yes."

"Sit down, then. You drop where you stand, I'm going to leave you there. Left my crane in my other suit. We alone?"

Ferris sat down in one graceless motion of descent, mashing the ugly cloth cushions beneath him like so much thin air, and said, "Yes. Completely."

"You don't have any girlfriends back there? Or boy-friends, maybe?" Gunner didn't mind stealing another comic's material, as long as it was sufficiently biting.

Ferris frowned. "Why would you ask that?"

"Pardon me?"

"You asked if I had a boyfriend back there. Were you trying to be funny, or were you implying something?"

He was actually miffed. As diplomatically as possible, Gunner said, "I was just trying to make sure we've got the place to ourselves. But if the way I phrased my question was suggestive of any buggery on your part, I apologize."

Ferris glared at him, cooled off, then started to swoon again. He was a man for all seasons, apparently.

"You killed Denny, didn't you?"

Gunner shook his head. "No."

"You were at the Y last Thursday. I saw you. In the locker room."

Gunner shrugged. "I'm an athletic kind of guy."

"Please. Don't joke."

"Look, Stan. You're confused. *I* called this meeting,

not you. I'm going to handle the questions and you're going to handle the answers. Okay?"

Ferris studied the black man's face for a moment before rolling his large head up and down several times, nodding.

"What makes you think Denny's dead?" Gunner asked him.

"I don't 'think' he's dead. I *know* he is."

"Okay. So how do you *know*? You see him fall down an open manhole or something?"

"I didn't see anything. And anybody who says I did is a liar." He was getting testy again. "But I haven't heard from Denny since I left his . . . since I talked to him on the phone Thursday morning. And he said then that somebody was trying to kill him. That's why he . . . I mean, why *I . . .*"

"The overnight bag. In the locker. I saw you make the drop, Stan, I know all about it. Go on."

Ferris was having a hard time keeping his hands still. He asked if he could have a cigarette, and Gunner consented, then watched him fumble through the process of drawing a pack of Winstons from his shirt pocket and lighting one with a book of stubborn matches.

"I went back to the Y that night to check the locker, to make sure he'd picked up his things. But he hadn't. He didn't show up to get them the day after that, either. And here it is, four days later, and I still haven't heard from him. So I figure he must have been right. It must have happened to him just the way he said it might."

"I don't suppose you'd know anything about why he was killed?"

Ferris shook his head.

"Or what he did to earn the money he gave you to drop his things off at the Y?"

"No."

"You didn't know he murdered two men in a bar three weeks ago?"

Ferris let out a long breath, blowing old smoke out so he could suck a lungful of new smoke in. "Denny wouldn't do that."

"He did it. And you helped him, you fat shit."

"No! I had nothing to do with it!"

Gunner grinned. "Then he *did* tell you."

The big head rocked up and down again, a piston of fat and bone. "He said he was the one who had killed that Buddy Dorris kid and the bartender. The Brother of Evolution, or Revolution, or whatever it is those crazy bastards call themselves. He told me, sure, but only after the fact. I'd have never let him do it otherwise, so help me."

"He tell you who put him up to it? Was it Larry Stewart, maybe?"

"Larry Stewart? Who's Larry Stewart?"

"I followed you here from Henshaw headquarters, Stan. You *work* for Larry Stewart."

"And you think Larry paid Denny to kill Dorris? You've got to be kidding."

"And if I'm not kidding?"

"Then you're crazy. No way Larry paid Denny to do anything. Absolutely no way." He was hoping that would be the end of it, but of course, it wasn't.

Gunner took a single step forward, toward him.

"I'm not crazy, Stanley. I'm just fresh out of time for fucking around." His voice had a hollow sound to it now, and he was wearing the face of a man on the edge of madness, one whose nerves felt like a frayed rope worn to a single strand. He was down to the last few hours of freedom Poole had tossed him like a bone, and he could no longer support a facade of indifference.

"How much did he get for the hit?"

"I don't know. Ten grand, I think. But that's all I know, I swear to God."

"Bullshit. If Townsend told you half the story, he told you all of it."

"No!"

"I was in his apartment when you packed his bag. I heard you looking for the Henshaw flyer in that little box of buttons on his dresser. You didn't find it because I found it first, but you knew what was on it just the same."

"No! I didn't know what Denny wanted with that fucking flyer!"

"You're lying, fat boy. And you're pissing me off. So I'm going to ask you one more time, before I start blowing your fingers off: *who paid Townsend to hit Buddy Dorris?*"

Ferris's eyes had locked onto the .357, a black metal serpent rearing its ugly head to strike. When at last he spoke, it was without actually hearing the words spill out of his own mouth.

"Larry. Denny said it was Larry."

Gunner felt his pulse take off, fear and exhilaration boiling together in the fuel that was his blood.

"But that's crazy, like I said! I didn't believe it when Denny first said it, and I don't believe it now. Larry's got a campaign to run, he's got no time to waste on thrill killings!"

"We're not talking about a thrill killing. We're talking about murder for hire."

"It doesn't matter what you call it! The Dorris kid and his hoodlum friends were no threat to Lew, they were just gnats on his ass. So why should Larry care if Dorris lives or dies? Dead or alive, who was he?"

On such short notice, Gunner couldn't say.

"Besides," Ferris went on, "Larry couldn't stand Denny. Wouldn't even speak to him, in fact. Since he joined the campaign in August, everyone else in the office had given Denny something to do at one time or another— run a note here, pick up a package there—but not Larry. Never Larry."

Gunner was reminded of Terry Allison's similar testimony. "And yet he kept Denny around."

Ferris didn't say anything.

"You didn't think that was odd?"

The big man shrugged. "Not really. Lew needs all the votes he can get, and Larry knows it. Although I'm sure he must have come pretty close to cutting Denny loose a number of times. For sure after . . ."

He stopped himself in mid-sentence, as if realizing he was about to tell an off-color joke in mixed company.

"After what?" Gunner said. It was an order to comply, not an innocent inquiry.

"After the drugstore thing," Ferris said.

Gunner encouraged him to be more specific with a determined silence.

Ferris burned a fresh hole in the right arm of the sofa crushing his cigarette out and said, "Denny and I made a run one Sunday to pick up a few emergency supplies. Stationery items the staff had to have and couldn't get from our normal supplier until Monday morning. We went to a Thrifty's, a couple blocks down from the office, and Denny started an argument with the cashier on our way out. He got all bent out of shape over the way she had handed me my change, or something dumb like that, and a couple of kids in the store took exception to some of his language. A security guard moved in to break things up and Denny just lost it.

"He busted the guard up pretty bad, and one of the bigger kids, too. Before I could talk him down, somebody called the cops, and they took us both in. We found out later it was Larry who eventually bailed us out and got the charges against Denny dropped."

"He didn't care for the publicity."

"No. At least, that's why we figured he'd done it. He never explained himself afterward, and that was fine by us."

"But he didn't let either of you go."

116

"No."

"The guard in the store. He was black, right?"

Ferris nodded reticently.

"And the kids? The cashier?"

Again, Ferris nodded, starting to see Gunner's point. "But that doesn't mean . . ."

"Save it, Stan. Stewart obviously liked what he saw. He was looking for somebody crazy enough to blow Dorris away for an attaboy and a few bucks, and he found one in his own backyard. I never met your pal Townsend myself, but from what I hear he would have been just what the doctor ordered: a moronic bigot with a short fuse and a pit bull's taste for blood."

"But they tried to kill him, Denny said. He got five grand up front, and was supposed to get five grand after, but when he went to collect, he was jumped by some guy in a ski mask. It was a set-up in a park somewhere, Denny said."

"Dead men tell no tales, man. What was Stewart supposed to do, trust Townsend not to sell his story to the *National Enquirer*?"

Ferris gave it some thought. He was no wiz with puzzles, but he had to admit Gunner's placement of the pieces made for a snug fit.

"Who *are* you?" he asked, finally. His cowardice was abating.

Gunner brought the fat man's attention back to the Police Special with a slight movement on his right hand and said, "I'm the man with the power, for a change. And it feels pretty good."

"Look. Let me go, huh? I've told you everything I know, I swear it."

Gunner shook his head. "Not yet, Stan. I haven't heard the why of it, yet."

"*Why*? Why what?"

"Why a man like Larry Stewart would go after a third-rate hell-raiser like Buddy Dorris. I need a reason. A motive. He didn't do it just for the fun of it, now, did he?"

"But I already told you—"

"Jack shit. That's what you told me. But then, I haven't taken your first finger off yet. Have I?"

As Gunner started toward him, someone at the back of the house opened a window.

Gunner managed to jump with some cool, but Ferris lacked that kind of self-control. The two of them looked off toward the dark abyss a hallway past the dining room opened onto, and waited for the warning sound of the window to be followed by another. Time only passed in silence.

"I thought you said we were alone," Gunner said, closing quickly on Ferris to take hold of his shirt collar and dead-lift the big man to his feet.

"I did! We are!"

The cold steel nose of the .357 came up under the white man's chin and Ferris took it as a hint to keep quiet. Together, the two men moved toward the back of the house, one leading the other along clumsily, and stopped halfway down the dark hallway, near an open door on the right that Gunner surmised led to one of two bedrooms. They waited there for a long moment, but again, all was silent; Ferris's labored breathing was the only sound in the air.

Gunner pushed his reluctant host forward and peered into the room ahead. He could see nothing clearly in its almost complete absence of light other than the window on the opposite wall. It was open fully and its outer screen was missing. The foul smell of salt water was growing in the little house, riding piggy-back on a limp breeze blowing in from the distant Pacific shoreline.

Gunner found the lights and turned them on.

Two men stood in the room only a foot or two from the door, facing him directly. One was slightly taller than he, with an upper body to match; the other was short and skinny, yet somehow more imposing than his friend. They wore silken black hoods wrapped tightly around their heads and were dressed in matching clothes of the common cat-burglar variety. The skin around their eyes the holes in their hoods could not conceal was two dissimilar shades of dark brown.

Gunner's first inclination was to empty his gun and hope for the best, but the drawback to that reaction was obvious: the big man on his left was holding a chrome-plated Browning automatic in one gloved hand, and all Gunner could see out of his left eye was its shiny, flat snout.

"Well, look who's here," the big man said cheerfully. "What a surprise."

Ferris made a whimpering sound and started to fold in Gunner's arms, passing out. He hit the floor like a bag of cement when Gunner let him go, too busy watching the Browning stare him down to do anything else.

Carrying a weapon of his own, the little man in the hood came forward to relieve the detective of the Police Special, and Gunner turned it over without resistance, saying nothing. He was trying to decide if he had ever heard the big man's voice before this moment.

"How the hell'd you get this?" the little man demanded, referring to the .357. Now Gunner had heard both men speak, but their voices were muffled behind the black hoods and it was all he could do to make out what they were saying.

"I found it in a trash can out in Hollywood," Gunner said, emotionlessly. "You don't remember putting it there?"

"Damn, Gunner. You are one determined mother-fucker," the larger man said, issuing the compliment with some amusement. "Anybody ever tell you that?"

Gunner wouldn't answer him.

"You've got what some people might call stick-to-itiveness. Which means you have no idea when to quit. Do you, smart ass?"

Still, Gunner wouldn't answer. The big man finally drew the Browning away from his face and gestured with it toward the front of the house. "Back to the living room," he said. "Now."

His cordiality was gone. He left his associate to take on the task of bringing Ferris around to rejoin them and led Gunner into the living room, using the Browning to coerce him into a seat at one end of the couch. The little man in the hall slapped Ferris with an open hand until the fat man was conscious again, then jostled and wrestled the stumbling giant into position beside Gunner.

"What the hell is happening?" Ferris asked, looking sick again.

"Shut the fuck up!" the little man told him, lackadaisically training the midnight special in his left hand upon him.

Watching Gunner closely, the big man said, "You're awful quiet, my man. Cat got your tongue?"

Gunner shrugged. "You have the floor, for now. Make the most of it."

The taller man's grin nearly shone through his disguise. "All right, then. I'll be brief. But I'd advise you to listen up, because this will be complicated. And I'm only going to recite it once." He shook his head. "You've been fucking up, Gunner. Left and right. You've been taking yourself and the Mickey Mouse job you do a little too seriously, and the party or parties my associate and I represent don't appreciate it. For them, you've become more trouble than you're worth. So the two of us have been asked to see what we can do about persuading you to back off for a while.

"Now. To achieve that effect we could kill you, of course. As a matter of fact, in retrospect, maybe that's what we should have done in the first place, considering all the good it did us to fix you up for Mr. Townsend's murder.

But we've decided we don't want to kill you. Seems we've come to like you, in a way.

"So what we're going to do, we're going to help you instead. We're going to make up for past transgressions and work something out that will hopefully prove beneficial to all concerned. You with me so far?"

Gunner didn't say one way or the other.

"I'll take that to mean you are. So here's the plan. You're going to wise up and walk away, Gunner. You're going to stop annoying my employers and live to tell about it. You're going to forget about Denny Townsend and Buddy Dorris, and you're going to forget you ever knew Buddy's sister Verna. You're going to go home and hide your face for a long, long time.

"Of course, in order to do that, you're going to have to get squared away with the authorities. But that's cool. Because we're going to fix that for you, too. With ease."

He took Gunner's handgun from the smaller man beside him and began to remove shells from the cylinder. "By the way. Has your buddy Ferris here told you what he *really* was to the late Denny Townsend? Or did he just give you that tired old 'we were the best of friends' horse manure?"

Ferris started to say something, but thought better of it. He looked to Gunner as if he could use another cigarette.

The big man in the hood glanced up to watch Ferris squirm, his hands still at work unloading Gunner's hefty .357. "Hell, they were banging buddies," he said, matter-of-factly. "They were partners in the crime of homo-you-know-what-is."

"That's a lie!" Ferris said.

"What they had was the real thing. An intense bonding of the souls, my sources tell me. But you know how those tempestuous romances can be. They run hot and cold. Tempers sometimes flare. Especially when there's a jealous hot-head like Stanley involved."

"That's a fucking lie! We were friends, that's all! Just good friends!"

The little man with the little gun stepped up to kick Ferris full in the mouth, like a ten-year-old bully imitating something he'd seen in a martial-arts movie. Ferris came out of it cheaply enough: he had a cut lower lip and a good reason to say nothing more.

"What I'm getting at," the larger man continued, as if blind to the interruption, "is that it just so happens that Ferris and his lover boy had one of their more impressive spats only days before the latter met his untimely death last Thursday. Ferris made some wild accusations and even threatened to do his beloved bodily harm. All in a *very* public place. And that means he had what, Mr. Private Investigator?"

"A motive," Gunner said, starting to squirm himself.

"That's right." The larger man reached out to hand Gunner's .357 back to the little man standing beside him and slipped its slugs into a trouser pocket. "So how does this story grab you: You went looking for Townsend and caught his spurned lover's attention in the process. The drop at the Y was his idea; he set it up and made sure you followed him there from Townsend's apartment so he could knock Townsend off and arrange things so you'd take the rap."

Ferris was asking for another kick in the mouth; he was shaking his head for all he was worth.

"What about him?" Gunner asked, nodding at the fat man on the opposite end of the couch. "That supposed to be his story, too?"

"Let me finish," the hooded one said.

"You mean there's more?"

"Oh, yeah. The happy ending. You look for the man who framed you for murder, and you find him. Here. But when you find him, he has a gun. Your gun. The one he shot Townsend with. Fortunately, being the wise man you are, you have a gun, too. This one." He had a second weapon in his hand now, an off-brand .38 with a long nose. "Can you guess the rest?"

Gunner could sense a wave of nausea coming on. His mouth was dry and his hands wouldn't stop shaking. "I kill him. In self-defense."

"That would be acceptable to us, yes. Or maybe he kills you in self-defense. Two men, two guns. Two bullets. These things are hard to call."

Ferris started to scream, but the shorter man in black was on top of him before he could get it going.

"Get him to his feet," the bigger man said, then turned to face Gunner again. "You too, hero."

Gunner didn't move. They were giving him a fifty-fifty chance to survive the night, and a chance like that was nothing to rush into.

"One more time," the man in the hood said, once more holding the Browning an inch from his face.

Gunner stood up.

The big man walked him over to the mouth of the hallway and turned him to face the living room again, where Ferris stood trembling a good nine yards away, the little pistol of his smaller unwanted guest pressed hard against his temple. He was crying. Gunner's Police Special was forced into Ferris's left hand as the off-brand .38 was forced into Gunner's right. They were made to hold the weapons loosely at their sides before the two men in black backed off, a few feet from each, the Browning pointed at Gunner's right eye, the midnight special at Ferris's left ear.

There was no doubt in Gunner's mind that Ferris would play the game straight. He wasn't strong enough to play it any other way.

"Go for it," the big man said abruptly.

The corpulent white man's arm came up at the word *go,* but Gunner's .38 spat a quick yellow flash and Ferris froze, his lifeblood suddenly spilling from a hole in his chest no larger than a quarter. He went down with a look of modest surprise growing hard on his face, a look Gunner knew he would see in his mind's eye for a long time to come.

"Aw, damn," the tall black man in the silken hood said to no one in particular. "You know what I think I did?"

"It wasn't loaded," Gunner said, without looking away from Ferris's prone body. He couldn't *make* himself look away.

"Yeah. Must have taken one too many bullets out of poor Stanley's gun, huh?"

He brought the butt of the Browning down hard upon Gunner's head and laughed. Gunner collapsed at the waist and started downward, fast.

It was a long fall to a far better world.

The blind nurse, who had sold her illegitimate baby to an ex-con employed by the hospital's linen delivery service before the speedboat accident that had claimed her sight, was paying a teenage babysitter to steal the infant back from its adopted parents when Ira Zeigler finally said, "Turn that shit off, Aaron, and listen to what I'm telling you."

Zeigler was Gunner's fifty-one-year-old lawyer and recalcitrant father figure, a man with no patience for inattentive clients and no taste for bad soap operas. Especially now. Only yesterday he had prostrated himself before a bail bondsman named Zero to get Gunner released from jail, using up a hefty favor he had been saving for a rainy day, and the black man was acting as if it were no big deal; as if $25,000 were a pittance Zeigler could beg off any one of a million friends without half trying.

Gunner turned off the TV.

"They've got you by the balls, kid. You know that."

"By the balls," Gunner said, nodding. It was almost two in the afternoon, and he was still dressed for bed.

"Manslaughter, maybe. Withholding evidence, for sure. Obstruction of justice. Two counts of breaking and entering, and one count of carrying an illegal firearm. That's just for starters. What they'll spring on you later, God only knows."

Gunner shrugged. "They'll think of something, I'm sure."

Zeigler glared at him. He had hard brown eyes set in deep pockets of flesh that could make a dust pile out of Mount Rushmore at a hundred and fifty paces. "All right, that's it. Cut the crap and tell me what's going on."

"Crap?"

"I want the truth, you smart-ass bastard. I want to know what happened, and how. Or am I supposed to be just as goofy as the cops are for buying that goddamned fairy tale you came up with?"

"It's no fairy tale, Ziggy. I just fucked up again, that's all. I got in a little over my head and made some poor decisions."

"*Poor* don't begin to cover it, kid. Try *masochistic*. Or *boneheaded*. Or both."

"Okay."

"You're telling me you let a fat bum like Ferris steal your gun and kill somebody with it. And that you in turn found another gun, broke into his home and killed *him* when he confronted you there."

"That's what I said, yeah."

"That's a load of shit!"

"Maybe you didn't hear me the first time. I said I fucked up."

"You fucked up, so you tell the police *everything*? Without talking to me first? I haven't taught you how to cover your ass any better than that?" Zeigler shook his head in wonder, red-faced. "You got any fruit in the box? An apple, maybe?"

He left the couch and headed for the kitchen. He was a physical fitness nut who spent as much of his time counting calories as he did bail money, and there was nothing his small, rock-hard frame could not do better or faster than those of many men half his age. Only the luminous bald spot at the back of his head was suggestive of his advanced years, and that was due more to worry for the low-lifes he habitually represented than the ravages of time.

When he returned from the kitchen to sit down again, he had an overly ripe pear in his hand. Gunner's place was a war zone and Gunner himself looked like a Skid Row reject, but Zeigler didn't say so. The kind of problems the black man had now, the Good Housekeeping seal would do little to fix.

"So that's how it's gonna be, huh? You want me to play it the way you laid it out?"

"I want you to make it as easy for me as you can, Ziggy. Keep my time in the joint under ten years and I'll be more than satisfied with your work."

"And your license to operate? To carry?"

"Fuck 'em. Unless they go after my license to drive, let 'em have whatever they want."

Zeigler eyed him again. "You've gotta eat, kid," he said.

"Hey, don't worry about me. Del's asked me back in the fold and I've told him I'm in, this time for good. We've all got to grow up sometime, right?"

Gunner smiled, but not painlessly. It was a difficult thing to do, treating Zeigler like a stranger, fair game for lies. For an old man whose name Gunner had found in the phone book over four years ago, he was a better friend to the black man than any Fairfax district shyster had a right to be.

"I don't want to see you go out this way, Aaron. Not through the back door with your tail between your legs."

"Let it go, Ziggy," Gunner said flatly.

"Somebody's scared you off. I can see that. I'm not

completely blind, yet. You're heading for the exits because you're afraid, not because you're tired of losing."

"Ziggy, Jesus Christ . . ."

"You know the first trick a dog trainer teaches a dog?" He took a bite out of his pear. "How to roll over. Not sit, like most people think. No. They teach it to roll over. And you wanna know why?" He leaned over in his chair, resting his elbows on his knees, and smiled complacently. "Because once you teach 'em that, the rest is *easy*."

Gunner's phone rang. Zeigler alone reacted, turning. Gunner didn't move.

"You gonna answer that?" Zeigler asked, taking another bite out of his pear.

Gunner shook his head. "The machine's on," he said.

After two rings, the phone fell silent.

"Where was I?" Zeigler wanted to know.

"You were leaving," Gunner said, getting to his feet. "Unless you have any questions I haven't already answered thirty times."

Zeigler stood up, briefcase in hand. "I could help you, kid, if you'd let me. I ever let you down before?"

"No."

"Then give me a chance to fight for you. Maybe there's nothing to be done about your license to carry, but we could maybe get 'em to settle for suspension of your license to operate, we play our cards right."

Gunner shook his head slowly and opened the front door for him. "Not worth the trouble, Ziggy. Thanks, anyway."

Zeigler couldn't understand it, the totality of Gunner's willingness to quit—but he went to the door without further complaint. Twenty-three years in the courtroom had taught him the difference between a case he could win and one any man would lose.

"I hope you're not making a mistake," he said.

Gunner put on a show of confidence, smiling again. "Not this time," he said.

Zeigler shrugged once and was gone.

As Gunner closed the door behind him the phone began to ring again. He moved to the answering machine atop a tall table in one corner of the living room and turned the volume up to screen the call. For the third time that day, the man on the end of the line was Brother Jamaal, Roland Mayes's personal video-historian.

"Gunner? You there? This is Jamaal Hill again. Listen, this is no joke. I've got something you need to see. Something of Buddy's. I don't know what it means, exactly, but I think it explains how he got himself killed, and by who. Understand? Give me a call, we'll get together somewhere. I want to do the right thing, man. You know what I mean?"

He left his number one more time and hung up.

Gunner pulled the phone jack out of the wall and proceeded to give the same bad soap opera one more chance to hold his attention.

Eleven pounds in three days. The Guilt Trip/Heat Wave Diet, Gunner called it.

What it was, was three days of confinement in the sun-blasted furnace his little house had become with only the beast of self-pity to keep him company. He was better off without the weight, and its absence should have made him lighter on his feet, but he had something more burdensome than body fat to lug from room to room now, and his ability to carry it was fast declining.

Guilt.

Del understood what was happening, as well as he possibly could. He was biding his time, letting Gunner come around at his own pace. He hadn't called since Thursday, one day after Gunner's strange hibernation began. Brother Jamaal, on the other hand, had called again today, but only once. Early. He was tiring, finally. Getting it through his head that it was time to quit. Just as Gunner had days ago.

Zeigler was doing a good job of making Gunner's improbable account of the events leading up to Stan Ferris's death hold water, and it looked as if the black man might spend the greater part of the following year on stiff probation rather than behind bars. Matt Poole had been no more awed by Gunner's testimony than Zeigler had, but he liked the straightforward way in which Gunner had laid the works out on his table, calling him in before Ferris's body was cold, and the homicide detective was doing his part to make things go a little easier for him. Anything not to have to hassle playing cat to someone else's mouse.

The TV was on twenty-four hours a day now, but it was just an excuse to have his eyes open. Gunner's mind was turned inward, locked in a closed loop. It was introspection of the most deadly order, a perpetual replay of limited images: fat Stanley Ferris falling to his living room floor, clutching a hole in his chest he could not believe was there; a tall man laughing behind a black silk mask; Denny Townsend in the dumpster he'd been tossed in, dead eyes aimed pointlessly skyward.

Guilt.

It was tearing him up from the inside out, making a mockery of his consciousness. Crushing his manhood down to size like a ball of tin foil in an iron fist. He had been used again, once more with fatal consequences; the game of make-believe he insisted on playing had exploded in his face anew. But this time there was a twist. This time he was helping.

Because that was better than being dead.

That was the important thing. He was alive. Haunted by shame and consumed with self-hatred, but alive and wiser for the experience. Better prepared to accept his limitations, both as a private investigator and a man. He had no business fucking around with incendiary men and institutions, political or otherwise. Small-time hoods and teenage punks were more in his league; against anything else, he was outmanned and outclassed.

Prudence, then, demanded that he quit while he still had his health, if not his pride. He would move on and learn to forget. He would persevere and seek peace of mind. Not because peace of mind would make him whole again, but because the only way to regain anything more for himself required that he strike back. Retaliate. Mere rationalizations would not work. He would have to resolve to shed blood and find some joy in it.

That was the catch.

He was convinced he had done all the killing he could do. In 'Nam or at home, directly or indirectly, it was all the same: dead was dead, and he was accountable. Viet Cong by the score, lying face up, face down, some with no faces at all: men, women, and children alike. A fourteen-year-old black girl named Audra Dobey, left butchered on a cot somewhere by an amateur-hour abortionist. Denny Townsend, blown open at the waist by a bullet from the detective's gun. And Stanley Ferris, last but not least, taking a header with an empty gun in his hand, the front of his shirt staining fast with blood, loser of a rigged duel.

They had all left spirits behind, and their spirits needed no company. His self-respect was simply not worth another ghost. And so his rage, what there was of it, would be stillborn; the human sacrifice it would take to resurrect his dignity would not take place.

He would survive, and leave it at that.

Survival was, after all, the most he felt he truly deserved.

Del's patience finally ran out on Monday, the fifth straight day of Gunner's self-imposed exile. He came to the door around four in the afternoon and wouldn't stop ringing the bell until Gunner answered it.

"You've got mail all over the porch," he said, handing over a stack of miscellaneous bills as he stepped inside.

The house was dark, the soft white face of Gunner's still-running TV set notwithstanding. A dirty sheet was falling from the couch to the floor, converting it from a broken-down piece of living-room furniture to an unkempt bed. The remains of several days-old meals stood drying on plates and dishes at various locations, the scent of bad luck bourbon hovering in the air like a black cloud with no silver lining.

Del took a moment to examine the wreckage, then turned his eyes of stone to Gunner and said, "Enough's enough. What the fuck's goin' on?"

It was a rhetorical question; he didn't wait for an answer. "I spoke with Ziggy this morning. To see if he could tell me why your phone's been out of order for the last two days. You know what he said? He said you've pulled the plug. On your *life*."

"Ziggy's been working too hard," Gunner said.

Del moved a plate of petrified lasagna and sat down in the room's one good chair. "You don't bullshit your attorney, Aaron. You tell him the truth, whatever the truth may be, and help him make a case out of it. That too much for Ziggy to ask?"

"I've told Ziggy what happened. A thousand times. If he chooses not to believe it, that's his problem."

"He's not stupid, man. He's been working for you for four years, you don't think he can tell when you're being straight with him and when you're not?"

"He's my lawyer, not my mother! I tell him what I want to tell him, goddammit!"

He was beginning to feel sick. The bile he had managed to suppress for four days was coming to the surface, and he was oddly relieved to sense it.

"And what about me?" Del asked. "That go for me, too?"

"It goes for everybody. Ziggy knows what he needs to know; you know what you need to know. I killed a man before he could kill me, and I'm through as a private investigator. The page has turned. I'm ready to go to work for you now, full time. What more do you want?"

"I want to believe you're making the break clean. That you're choosing this moment to get out and go in with me because that's what you want, not because you're afraid. Afraid of what you've done, or what you might do again, if you don't."

"Look. It's time, that's all. You don't think it's time?"

"What *I* think doesn't matter. If you think it's time, then it must be. But don't kid yourself, and don't kid me— you can't turn your back on ten years' work out of fear and expect to make it stick."

Gunner laughed. Del could usually be relied upon to see through a man with disarming precision, but this time he had it all wrong. Gunner was afraid, that much was true—but not *of* himself.

For himself.

"I say something funny?"

Gunner kept laughing, unable or unwilling to stop. He had a bottle of Lord Calvert in his hand and was pouring himself a drink, a large one in a dirty glass.

"You overestimate me, cousin," he said, grinning, before tossing the bourbon down in a rush.

Del took a good hard look at him, already fast at work on a second drink, and said, "Maybe I do."

He went to the door and opened it. Terry Allison was standing on the other side, out on the mail-strewn porch, getting ready to ring the bell. They both did a double-take, surprised.

"I'm looking for Aaron Gunner," the blond said stiffly, breaking their shared paralysis first. She was wearing a light cotton summer dress in pastel blue, sleeveless and scoop-necked to expose all the perfectly bronzed flesh she could legally afford to display. The garment itself was innocent; the firm, lithe body beneath it was not.

Del turned to Gunner for help, at a loss for words. Gunner walked his fresh drink over to the door and greeted Allison with a crooked smile, going out of his way to make her feel cheap and out of place.

"Well. Will wonders never cease." He turned to his cousin and said, "Del, this sweet young thing is Ms. Terry

Allison, right-hand lady of would-be Congressman Lew Henshaw's right-hand man, Larry Stewart. Say hello to my cousin Del, Ms. Allison."

Allison nodded and took Del's hand, making a feeble attempt to shake it.

"Ms. Allison thinks Lew Henshaw is just what her district needs, Del. Maybe, somewhere down the road, just what we all need. If you know what I mean."

"That's not why I'm here, Mr. Gunner," Allison said, blushing, tainting her tan with a faint crimson glow.

"No?"

"No."

"Ah. You must've heard about your pal Ferris, then. You want to ask me not to waste any more of your delivery boys, I guess."

"No! If you'd just listen to me for a second—"

"Waitaminute, waitaminute. I've got it. If it's not Henshaw, and it's not Ferris, then it must be something kinky that brings you all the way out here, into the *ghet-to*. You want to know if what they say about us is true, right? You want to find out first-hand whether or not we're just as good in the sack as we are on the dance floor."

"Aaron, Jesus, man," Del said.

Gunner wouldn't take his eyes off the girl. "Hey, no problem. I can spare a few minutes. Del was just leaving. Weren't you, Del?"

Allison ran off. She fumbled her way into a late-model white-on-white Toyota Supra parked at the curb out front and peeled some tread off its tires pulling away. Gunner stepped out onto the porch to watch her go and laughed, his voice ringing more with melancholy than amusement.

Del came up beside him and said, "Up until a few minutes ago, I was only guessing. But now I'm sure." He paused. "Whatever it is you're trying to forget, it's not going to go away. It's going to fuck with you until you die, or until you deal with it. One or the other." He shook his head. "You're not ever going to be able to outrun it."

Gunner grinned and finished off his drink. "Watch me," he said.

He went back inside the house and closed the door behind him.

The last Thursday in October, ten days after his arrest in connection with the death of Stanley Ferris, Gunner started his second term of employment under his cousin Del, making his retirement from private investigation official. With two hundred-plus hours of uninterrupted self-pity under his belt, he stepped back into the light of day like a man emerging from an extended coma and endeavored to learn all over again the ways of the living.

The heat wave that had tortured Los Angeles for five consecutive weeks was at last abating, freeing the mercury in a million thermometers to dip below ninety and settle there, but some people were slow to notice the change. They still had to squint against a white-hot sky and drive their cars with the windows rolled down; their throats remained dry and it still hurt to breathe and their clothes continued to cling to their bodies like a wetsuit. The meteorological crisis that had driven them to the edge of anar-

chy was over, but its effects lingered on. The human time
bomb Black America had become was still ticking, and
would for a few days more, at least.

Meanwhile, Gunner went about his business as a re-
born electrician's apprentice with relative peace of mind.
The Buddy Dorris affair was behind him. His phone had
been plugged back in since early Tuesday and had yet to
ring. Brother Jamaal had given up the ghost and Verna
Gail had apparently never really given a damn in the first
place, so that was that. He was making his break for a better life, and there were no more voices of dissent to be
heard. He was home free.

His first day on the job went well. He spent a short
four hours helping Del install a new AC outlet in a Century
City office computer room, took a long lunch, and was
summarily dismissed until Friday.

And then Al Dobey turned up.

Gunner was walking a forty-dollar bag of groceries
home from the Alpha Beta market on Florence and Central
when he spotted the portly pimp coming out of a barber
shop across the street. A fresh shave and haircut made him
look less the sleazeball than usual, but there was no mistaking the three diamonds in Dobey's left earlobe or the pre-
scription sunglasses under his panama hat. He looked up
from a wad of money in his right hand as he hit the sidewalk and caught sight of Gunner across the way. He shoved
the money into his right-hand trouser pocket, then started
to run.

Like a sprinter reacting to the starter's gun, Gunner
took off after him, giving no thought to what he was doing.
Forty dollars' worth of food just hit the ground and he was
gone, legs pumping at full tilt, arms swinging back and
forth in alternate rhythm.

Dobey's fat was a definite impediment to his progress,
but his fear was great enough to counteract it. Without his
hat, lost in the first ten feet of his flight, he was moving like
a man thirty pounds lighter and ten years younger. No

sooner had Gunner joined him on the north side of Florence than the pimp crossed back to the south side, running
west toward Wadsworth, rebounding off a Japanese pick-up
that never hit its brakes, and weaving his way around several other vehicles that did. Gunner followed suit, but with
greater care, allowing Dobey to claim a sizable lead.

Dobey restricted the chase to Florence, refusing to
veer off in one direction or another and abandon the myr-
iad distractions and obstructions the heavily populated boulevard had to offer. It was difficult terrain for both men to
traverse, and that was to Dobey's advantage. The street
was full of people, young and old, male and female, moving grudgingly or not at all. Maybe someone the pimp
shoved out of his way would disapprove of Gunner trying
the same trick moments later, and would lodge a vehement
protest with a loaded gun or a sharp knife. Maybe Gunner
would nudge the wrong woman's child, or step on the
wrong man's foot. It wouldn't take much to get killed today; it never did.

None of this was of much concern to Gunner, however. His mind was on other things. Like breathing and
keeping his balance, and ignoring the pain in his still-aching
ribs, all the while trying to decide what it was he was doing,
and why, or for whom, he was doing it. Dobey was a valid
foe only in Gunner's old world, his surrendered world; he
held no meaning in the present one. Taking the pimp in his
hands and changing the shape of his face forever would accomplish nothing. It would not bring back Audra Dobey. It
would not make Gunner's past any less a disaster.

So what the hell was he doing?

Dobey had put thirty yards between himself and his
pursuer when he reached the intersection of Avalon and
Florence and came to a halt. He had gone as far as his fear
could take him, and he was tired. His lungs were burning
and his powder-blue suit was dark with sweat. He reached
behind his back to pull a nine-millimeter Beretta from the

waistband of his pants and waited patiently for Gunner to break from the crowd before him.

In his excitement, Dobey had failed to notice the black-and-white Dodge sitting to his left on the opposite side of Florence on Avalon, where two uniformed policemen were giving a kid on a moped a hard time for parking in a red zone. Gunner, however, had been more attentive; he was now ensconced in a snug little break between two buildings, out of harm's way. Dobey was waiting for him in vain.

The mass of people in line with the pimp's Beretta broke off in all directions as those who had seen it dove for cover and those who had not instinctively did likewise, anyway. By the time Dobey saw the two men in blue racing across Florence toward him, he was alone on the corner with nowhere to run and no cover to take. A sitting duck.

"Halt! Police!"

They only let him hear it once. They let him turn in their direction and gave him a full second to drop the Beretta before cutting him down, making the choice for him. They fired six rounds each, emptying their weapons; then and only then did they leave the street to approach his body, what little remained to bloody the ground.

Like most uniformed cops assigned to this part of the city, both men were Caucasian, razor sharp and humorless. The younger of the two went to call for back-up while his partner stayed behind to look Dobey over. He was down in a crouch, rifling the dead pimp's pockets, when it dawned on him that a crowd was gathering around him, and the gun in his holster was empty. He stood up slowly and glanced about, his left hand searching for the nightstick at his waist.

"All right, people, let's break it up."

"Say what?" someone asked.

"Break what up?" someone else demanded.

"You shot that man in cold blood," a woman said.

"Sure as hell did," a young boy agreed. "I seen it."

The cop held his ground. "Let's go. Move it, I said!" He had his baton out now. He craned his neck to see how the kid at the car was coming along, but the crowd was blocking his view. Traffic was starting to back up on the street as drivers paused in the middle of the intersection to watch the growing mob on the sidewalk.

Gunner had come out of hiding and was moving toward the shrinking circle where the cop was making his stand beside Dobey's body. The black man could see what was coming and felt obligated to stop it, having no desire to be the imbecile credited with striking the first match in the Second Torching of Los Angeles.

"He ain't got no bullets in his gun," someone said in a shrill, animated voice. "It was clickin', remember?"

"That's right. I heard it," a tall man wearing a red headband said, standing in the front row. "He fired six times, then nothin'." He started to smile.

"Bullshit," Gunner said, on a hunch. He, too, was in the front row now, directly opposite the man in the headband. "It was the other one shot six times. This man here, he only shot four times."

"Four times? You're crazy!"

"His motherfuckin' gun was *clickin'*" the shrill voice said again, behind the big man.

Gunner shook his head. "That wasn't *his* gun. That was his partner's. I was standing right here. I saw the whole thing. This guy only shot four times. You don't believe me, go ahead and fuck with him, see if he doesn't put two bullets in your ass. You think you've got a high voice now . . ."

The crowd broke up. Gunner grinned. The younger policeman reappeared, riot gun in hand, as sirens began to assert themselves in the distance.

"You okay?" the kid asked his partner, confused by the laughter of the gathering. The older man nodded and stole a glance in Gunner's direction, saying thanks the only way he could.

Two more black-and-whites lurched to a halt at the curb, having crossed the double yellow line bisecting Florence against traffic, and the party was over. While the mass of black people surrounding the two uniformed officers began to dissipate, a small, middle-aged, pock-marked man in a knitted cap stepped forward to get one last look at Gunner before moving on. He didn't seem impressed.

"Funny man," he said, frowning.

The shrill voice Gunner had ridiculed was his.

The demon, it seemed, had been exorcised, the dragon slain.

The key figure in Gunner's darkest recurrent nightmare had resurfaced after eight months in hiding, slammed into a wall of pistol fire, and changed Gunner's life in the process. The man Gunner had been and the man he was now, now that the book on Al Dobey could be closed forever, were two distinctly different people. That much he could sense; that much was clear.

Initially, Gunner thought himself merely drunk with self-satisfaction, high on a long-standing bloodlust finally satiated, but he quickly realized there was more to his catharsis than that. He was not above finding some justice in Dobey's death—the debt he owed the pimp's daughter had to be from this moment on considered paid in full—but Dobey's death itself, it seemed to Gunner, was not what had done the trick. The pimp's fate was immaterial. What he had awakened just by showing his face again was not.

It had taken Gunner over a week of seclusion to convince himself that his manhood was not worth fighting for, that his pride was a luxury he could easily do without, but Dobey had lain such assumptions to waste in a matter of seconds. Had Gunner let him go when he first started to run, granted him escape uncontested, it would have been impossible to ever again second-guess his decision to trade private investigation for Del's offered partnership. But he had taken off after the pimp instead. The self-respect he had given up for dead had some life in it after all.

Which meant there were new decisions to be made, and little time to make them.

Gunner came to understand all this in the dark, displaced ruins of his living room early Thursday evening, after the smoke had cleared on his busy day. With all the windows open and the curtains drawn shut, the front of the house was almost bearable. He was propped up on the couch with slippers on his feet and nothing but Calvins under his robe, letting an old Bob James album on the stereo massage the kinks out of his mood.

While his mind sought to assimilate fifteen thoughts at once, he absently sorted through the pile of unopened mail he had collected over his several days of social withdrawal and came upon one parcel in particular that stood out from the rest. It was a brown-papered rectangle only slightly larger than a paperback book, with sharp-edged corners and flat, unremarkable surfaces. Gunner took it in his hands and looked it over, guessing its weight to be somewhere around a pound. Someone with a steady hand and a good calligrapher's pen had addressed it, but had left no clue to its origin other than a Los Angeles postmark of the previous Friday.

With little fanfare, Gunner peeled the package open to find a video cassette of the VHS variety, devoid of labels or markings of any kind. It shared its case with a short note on lined paper, another fine example of someone's flair for calligraphy, which read: "Buddy had me take this. I think he'd want you to see it."

Brother Jamaal's name was at the bottom of the page, along with the phone number he had left on Gunner's answering machine half a dozen times the previous week. He had been smart to include it; Gunner had erased his earlier messages days ago. Gunner moved to the phone and tried dialing his number now, but the line only rang monotonously in his ear. He got up to find his wallet, came back to the phone, and dialed a different number, this one scrawled in an indelicate hand on the back of a green campaign flyer.

It would be a call worth making only if Terry Allison was a big enough lady to forgive and forget—and knew how to get her hands on the right type of VCR on extremely short notice.

A young, clean-shaven black man with impeccable taste in clothes was seated behind the wheel of a parked car, waiting for something to happen. It was dark, well into night on a residential street that was both quiet and undistinctive. Gunner had never seen the man before, but the car was a definite flash from the past: a bronze BMW with a factory rim in the rear and a chrome wheel up front, both on the driver's side. He had to give it some thought, but in time he remembered why it was familiar: it was the same car he had admired in the drive-through line of the hamburger stand next to Boulos Kasparian's ARCO station, only hours before someone used his gun to send Denny Townsend on his way to the Great Beyond.

"You know him?" Gunner asked Terry Allison.

Allison shook her head, her eyes fixed on the screen of her bedroom TV. She had taken Gunner's late call to Henshaw campaign headquarters after a typically long day, and had played hard to appease until they both got tired of haggling and she agreed to a rendezvous at her Pacific Palisades home. "You?"

Gunner turned back to the screen himself. "No."

Time passed. Ten minutes went by and the BMW driver's image began to waver slightly, betraying the restlessness of the cameraman across the street. He, too, was seated in a parked car; glimpses of its interior kept cropping up as he regularly steadied himself. The black man in the BMW reached forward for something, then straightened back up. There was no sound to prove it, but he must have turned the radio on; his left hand started tapping away on the wheel in front of him.

Without warning, the camera eye swung right, to the BMW's rear, and focused on a big gray Lincoln pulling over to park behind it, one house down. A tall white man in a solid brown sweatsuit got out and started for the black man's car, a tan leather attaché case in one hand. He looked to be in his early forties, in good shape but balding; the hair at the top of his head was fading fast, and the hair on either side was feathered with gray.

"Jesus," Allison said. "That's Larry."

The tall man made it over to the BMW and got in on the passenger side. Brother Jamaal zoomed in as best he could, but from this distance there was no way to be sure about anything, other than the fact that the two men were on friendly terms. They chatted long enough to tell a short riddle each and that was it. Larry Stewart went back to his Lincoln and drove off, leaving his attaché case behind. His friend in the BMW performed an illegal U-turn moments later and effected his own retreat. The tape ended abruptly soon afterward.

Allison was in a state of shock. Gunner waited for Brother Jamaal's tape to rewind before subjecting her to any questions.

"You're sure that was Stewart?" he asked finally.

She nodded and, tired of staring at it, turned off the TV.

"But you've never seen the other guy before?"

"No. Never." She looked at him for the first time.

"Any idea what might have been in the case?"

"Twenty-five thousand dollars."

There didn't seem to be any doubt in her mind.

"How would you know that?" Gunner asked.

"I've been going over the books at the office. Somebody's been playing with the figures, and that's how much is missing. I couldn't believe Larry took it before, but now . . ."

She turned away again.

"That why you came to see me last week? When I made such an ass of myself?"

"I had nowhere else to go," Allison said, angrily. "I didn't want to go to the police. Not yet. I was afraid I might be wrong, and I couldn't afford to be wrong. There were too many careers at stake, too many *lives* at stake."

"Could you tell where that scene took place? Or when it might have happened?"

"Not where. But I might be able to help you with the when. Larry doesn't own that Lincoln anymore. He sold it late last month. He drives a Z now."

"A Datsun?"

"Nissan. They're called Nissans now."

Gunner nodded. "Yes, of course. My mistake."

He took his rewound tape out of Allison's machine and gave her every indication that he was leaving immediately. His adrenaline was running on the main pump again.

"What are you going to do?" Allison asked. "You're not going to the police?"

"No. I'm not going to the police." He gave her an imploring look. "And neither are you. Understand?"

"I want to know what you plan to do," she said, firmly. Her arms were crossed, constricting the delicate breasts beneath the white silk blouse she was wearing in a manner that did not escape Gunner's notice, preoccupied as he was.

"I don't know. Drop in on the man who made this tape, for starters. After that, I have no idea." He laughed, suddenly. "Why? You worried about me?"

She didn't so much as smile at the thought. "Do you think I'm a bigot, Mr. Gunner?"

The question was meant to be answered earnestly.

"I think you have all the makings of a great one," Gunner said. "But I'd say you're not that far gone, yet."

"I guess you think I have a lot to learn."

The black man surveyed her openly and smiled, his appreciation for her pristine beauty difficult to conceal in the woman's own bedroom.

"About some things, yes."

"Perhaps if I made a greater effort to interact with different kinds of people, I'd be less prone to make false judgments about them."

"Interaction would help, yeah. What kind did you have in mind?"

She sat down at the foot of her bed and kicked off her shoes. They were soft leather pumps in a pleasant navy blue. "Not what you're thinking," she said. "Although anything's possible, I suppose."

"You think maybe I could enlighten you to some things regarding my people. Is that it?"

"Couldn't you?"

"If I thought it would do some good, sure. But I wouldn't have to lay you to do it. The things I think you need to learn, you can't learn on your back."

"Good."

"Or in any other carnal position, for that matter."

"Fine."

"But over a candlelit dinner in another part of the house, if I should manage to get out of this mess I'm in alive . . ." He paused and shrugged. "Anything's possible."

They both laughed nervously at that, for a moment which quickly passed. Then Gunner excused himself and departed, before he could give much thought to the golden opportunity he was flatly kissing good-bye.

Jamaal Amir Hill had a thing for the La Brea Tar Pits.

It had taken four calls, but Gunner had finally reached the Brother of Volition at home late Thursday night. They spoke on the phone only long enough to agree that a meeting between them was in order, and Gunner graciously allowed the younger man to name a neutral site to his liking. Hill chose the Tar Pits, the prehistoric graveyard and popular historical park adjacent to the Los Angeles County Museum of Art in the heart of Wilshire Boulevard's decaying Miracle Mile. He wasn't just being creative; he had an affection for the place he made obvious by being early, even though Gunner had called for an 8 A.M. Friday arrival time.

A moist sheen of morning dew was burning off the grass throughout the park when Gunner found him, taking in the life-and-death struggle between the largest pool of raw petroleum on the grounds and a stone mastodon caught in its grasp, as if he had yet to catch on that the beast in the pit was a fake. Gunner joined him at the waist-high railing surrounding the pool and Brother Jamaal didn't object, seemingly unaffected by his arrival.

"He's not going anywhere," Gunner said, appraising the languid scene himself.

Without turning, Hill said, "Not that one, no. But maybe there's one still down there somewhere that is." He pointed. "I mean, *look* at that shit."

He was referring to the tar. It was infinitely opaque, viscous, and deep; scattered bubbles popped into slow-moving ripples on its surface and bands of color glistened to betray its oily base. A leaden saber-toothed tiger stood across the way, opposite the mastodon and just as hope-lessly mired in the muck.

"You think they'll ever know for sure what's down there and what isn't? Hell no. They can dig for a thousand years and still not know." Hill laughed. "That's why I love this place, man."

He faced Gunner finally, said, "Drives white people crazy, not knowin' all there is to know about somethin'. Havin' to guess and wonder gives 'em the creeps."

"There's a name for that," Gunner said dryly.

"Yeah? What's that?"

"Fear of the dark. It means you don't like mysteries. Or people who beat around the bush."

He wasn't trying to be funny; he was just passing along a heavy hint that he *was* in a hurry.

"You know the white man on the tape?" Hill asked, brusquely. "The cat drivin' the Lincoln, with the case?"

Gunner nodded.

"How about the brother in the Bimmer? You know him?"

"No."

"But I bet you'd like to, huh?"

Gunner didn't say anything. Hill grinned. "His name is

Price," he said. "Jimmy Price. He's a lawyer and tax man, works for Lou Jenkins exclusively."

"Sweet Lou Jenkins?"

"Yeah. Sweet Lou. King Pimp himself. Price is his lawyer and also his boy, just like Mouse is Roland's. Some people just have to have one, I guess."

"Damn."

Gunner was thinking about Lilly Tennell, and how hard it was going to be to apologize for his stubborn insistence that she was a moron for having mentioned Buddy Dorris and Lou Jenkins in the same breath.

"Surprised?" Brother Jamaal asked.

Gunner shook his head and said, "I don't see the connection. Between Jenkins and Stewart. Or was Price hooking up with Stewart on his own that night?"

Hill shook his own head. "Uh-uh. No way. He was acting as Sweet Lou's second, same as he always does."

"And Stewart?"

"Stewart was acting for himself."

"Or Lew Henshaw," Gunner said.

Hill shrugged. "Possibly. But not likely. Sweet Lou didn't go to school with Lew Henshaw." He smiled. "But he and Stewart were teammates on the varsity lacrosse team at Syracuse University, class of '72. I know. I've seen the yearbook."

Gunner gave his next question some thought, stalling for time to avoid looking as confused as he felt. "So they took a glorified gym class together, so what? Fifteen years is a long time. Those two have done a lot of parting of the ways since then. Stewart's a white supremacist in Republican's clothing and Jenkins is a semi-respectable gangster. What the hell could a pair like that want with each other now?"

"You're the detective," Hill said. "Go ask Roland."

"Mayes? What's Mayes got to do with it?"

It had all *started* with Mayes, Brother Jamaal said. Mayes and Sweet Lou Jenkins.

The two had never had any dealings in the past—they were polarized by the conflicting nature of each's influence on the black community—but back in the latter part of July, Jenkins had suddenly made it known he wanted to call a truce, to meet with Mayes personally in order to discuss what he called "matters of mutual interest." Buddy Dorris couldn't see where the Brothers of Volition and a mild-mannered pusher of "soft" narcotics could *have* any areas of mutual interest, but Mayes, oddly open to Jenkins's overtures, disagreed, and the tryst eventually took place over dinner the third week in August. Jenkins brought his man Price; Mayes matched Price with Dorris.

"Roland and Lou came out of the meetin' havin' made a pact of some kind, and Buddy didn't like it," Brother Jamaal remembered. "He came to me a few days later, lookin' for help. He told me all hell was about to break loose, that the Brothers were gonna get fucked unless he could convince Roland to renege on the deal he'd struck with Sweet Lou."

"He tell you what the deal involved?"

"No. He didn't want me or anyone else to know. All he'd say was that Sweet Lou couldn't be trusted, that his motives and ours could never peacefully coexist, and that we had to find a way to make Roland see that, fast, before the Brothers went the way of all the other black-power movements before us."

He shrugged again, this time apologetically. "So I agreed to help however I could. Not because I believed his story particularly—or had any reason to doubt Roland's leadership—but because I knew no matter what the truth was, Buddy's priorities were the same as mine: the Brothers first, and everything else second. Always."

"So you started following Lou's boy around," Gunner said.

Hill nodded. "To see if maybe we could figure out

what he and Lou were up to, yeah. We'd take turns tailin' him, sometimes alone, sometimes together, but always with the camcorder. We knew he'd be the one to watch—Lou doesn't do any of his own grunt work—so we stuck with him, day and night. From his sweet little Inglewood condo to Lou's Kitchen in Lynwood, and everywhere else in between. The first five days we could've just as soon stayed at home—but on the sixth, we got lucky.

"He left the Kitchen around eight that night, had a late dinner in Marina Del Rey, then drove out to Manhattan Beach. He took that coastal road, Vista Del Mar, all the way, drivin' slow, takin' his time. We thought he was just goin' for a little after-dinner cruise until he pulled off the main drag and started movin' through the residential district, away from the water. He parked his car on a street called Agnes Road and just sat there inside, waitin'. Around a quarter after ten, you-know-who showed up, and you saw the rest. Stewart deliverd a payoff of some kind. Right?"

"That would be my guess, yeah," Gunner said.

"That's what Buddy and I thought, too," Brother Jamaal said. "But neither of us could figure out what it could be a payoff for, or how it might relate to Lou's deal with Roland, until Buddy did some checkin' into Stewart's background and came up with the yearbook. He seemed to have the whole picture clear in his mind after that, only he wouldn't share it with me. He told me just to hang onto the tape for him and be cool, that he'd straighten everything out and get back to me if he needed it."

"But he never did."

"No. A week later, he was dead. Everybody said a crazy had killed him, one more fucked-up white man tryin' to throw a wrench into the machine, and it was easier to accept that explanation than to deal with the possibility that Roland or Sweet Lou had had him killed. So I pretended to believe it. And I think I almost did, until you showed up and started askin' people a lot of questions I should have had the guts to ask myself."

"*¡Cuidado! ¡La pelota!*"

Off to Gunner's right, a red rubber handball escaped a handful of Mexican children playing nearby and bounded over the railing into the black tar, landing about six feet from the edge of the pit. There were eleven people standing at the railing in all, including the recently arrived father of the children to whom the ball belonged, but no one moved to the toy's rescue. No one, apparently, was that crazy.

"Anybody know about the tape besides you and Buddy?" Gunner asked Hill, as someone finally ran off to find a park attendant.

Brother Jamaal shook his head. "Not unless Buddy told somebody about it, no. You're the only one I've told."

"And there's only the one copy?"

"Yes."

"You're sure?"

"I'm positive. Why?"

"Because somebody's been trying to find it, I think. They tore up Buddy's apartment rooting around for it, maybe last week some time. They haven't tried your place yet?"

Hill shook his head again. "We weren't tight, me and Buddy. Not with each other, not with anybody. We only got together for this deal the one time, and that only out of necessity. Nobody's figured us for a team yet, I guess."

"That's good," Gunner said, nodding his head pensively. "That means you've still got a little time."

"Yeah? For what?"

Gunner turned a hard smile in his direction. "To live," he said, matter-of-factly. "What else?"

Red lips on an ugly face. That was Lilly.

"Oh, you believe me now, huh? About Sweet Lou wantin' to kill J.?"

"I have reason to believe Sweet Lou may have been involved in J.T.'s death, yes."

"You've come to tell me you're sorry, then. For not listenin' to somebody when they try to tell you somethin'."

"I'm sorry, Lilly. Really."

"Uh-huh. You're sorry, all right. You and Howard both."

J.T.'s widow scowled, lighting a fresh cigarette. The sign in the window said the Acey Deuce was open for business, but no one seemed to want to believe it. Just a few minutes early for the noon rush, Gunner and a mammoth man of the cloth were the only customers in the place. The parson was squeezed into a booth near a window looking onto the street, and Gunner was at the bar, grilling Lilly.

"So now you believe me, you gonna do anything about it?" the large black woman asked. "Or do I have to hire you for that? Like somebody who wasn't fillin' your glass three times a week for free, not so long ago?"

"You don't have to do anything but stop bitching for five minutes and answer a few questions," Gunner said. "You feel up to that?"

"Yeah. I feel up to it. What do you wanna know?"

"I want you to tell me again about that phone call you say J.T. received from Lou Jenkins's man Jimmy Price. I want you to try to remember everything you may have overheard."

Lilly told the story again, although it seemed even thinner the second time around. Someone had called the Deuce looking for J.T. several days before his death, and Lilly had answered the phone. An articulate young black man she could only assume was Price asked to speak to her husband regarding their "recent dialogue at the Kitchen," Jenkins's Lynwood restaurant and base of operations, and the ensuing conversation between the two men had been an ugly one. J.T. took the call behind closed doors and exploded, cursing like a madman, making wild threats. Most of what he said was unintelligible from where Lilly was forced to try and make it out, on the other side of an insulated wall and closed office door, but one thing, at least, was not: J.T. did not want Price or Lou Jenkins anywhere near his place.

"'You motherfuckers stay away from my place!' J. kept sayin','" Lilly recalled, getting the attention of the parson in the booth by the window without particularly wanting it. "Over and over. 'Stay the fuck away from my place, or I'll have the police on your ass!'"

"But he never mentioned Price or Jenkins by name," Gunner said.

"No."

"Or the Deuce?"

The question took Lilly by surprise. She mulled it over for a moment, then shook her head. "No. I don't think he ever said 'the Deuce,' specifically—now that you mention it."

Gunner did some ruminating of his own before asking, "You ever see Price or Jenkins come in here? Would you know them if you served them?"

"Yeah, I'd know. You can't live and work in this community without comin' face-to-face with those two, 'ventually. They're goddamn institutions."

"But they've never been to the Deuce that you know of."

"No."

"How about the Kitchen? You or J.T. ever visit the Kitchen?"

Lilly shrugged. "A couple times. Once for dinner, once for lunch."

"J.T. ever go there alone?"

"I don't know. Maybe."

Gunner paused. "Can you think of any reason Jenkins might have to want to buy into the Deuce? Either partially or outright?"

Lilly shook her head. "No. This is a bar, baby, not a gold mine."

And Jenkins couldn't have been looking to open a new distributorship in the area: unless he had lost his lease, the record store only two blocks north on Vermont was his, lock, stock, and barrel, and anyone who wasn't deaf, dumb, and blind knew it, the local authorities included.

"Then maybe J.T. wasn't talking about the Deuce," Gunner said.

Lilly started to ask him what he meant, but the door to the bar opened and someone invited himself in, catching her eye. It was Little Pete, the neighborhood hot-weapons merchant, a man whose diminutive size made "Little" seem too generous a name for him. Dressed like a Depression-era pencil salesman and sporting a face he refused to shave more than once a week, he looked as insolvent as ever.

"You're late," Gunner said.

"My mornin' appointment ran long," Little Pete said, coming closer. He could just see over the counter of the bar without standing on his tippy-toes. "How you doin', Lilly?"

"I'm doin' fine, Junior. And I'm gonna keep on doin' fine, providin' you ain't brought no shit in here."

"Who? Me? Carry firearms on my person? Never. That's illegal, sister."

"Have a drink and sit down a minute, Pete," Gunner said, gesturing for Lilly to set the tiny man up at the far end of the bar. "I'll be right with you."

Little Pete nodded casually and followed Lilly to a distant stool, which he managed to climb before the bartender had intuitively filled the glass sitting there with the libation of his choice, Johnny Walker Red and Seven-Up. Perhaps feeling ignored, the Deuce's only other customer, the overweight parson in the window booth, got up and walked out, and Lilly neither stopped him nor said good-bye.

"What's he doin' here?" the big woman asked Gunner upon her return, tilting her head in Little Pete's direction. "He have somethin' you need, all of a sudden?"

"Let's just say I don't feel safe in this world running

around with just a comb in my pocket," Gunner said. "If
that's all right with you."

Lilly shrugged. "It's your ass."

"That's right. It is." He gave Little Pete a quick glance
and went on. "Now. As I was saying. If Jenkins was after
some place of J.T.'s, but the Deuce was of no use to him
that we can see, then maybe he wasn't after the Deuce at
all. Maybe he was after something else. Some *place* else."

"Some place else? Like what? Where? The Deuce is
all we've got that's worth anything." She paused. "I mean,
the *market* ain't worth nothin' . . ."

She was looking past him at the rear of the club, seeing
something that wasn't really there.

"What market?" Gunner asked.

"J. bought it, last year some time. That old boarded-
up Vons market on Manchester and Hoover, across from
the fire station. He was gonna make one of those super-
stores of liquor out of it, he said, if we could ever scrape up
enough money to get it into shape."

"J.T. bought that dump?"

"Yeah. Real estate and J. never did mix too well, God
bless the fool."

"Anybody been using it, that you're aware of? Are
you leasing it out, or anything like that?"

Lilly shook her head. "Are you kiddin'? What's anybody gonna use it for? Ain't nothin' in there but some
shelves and stuff. I went there once right after J. bought it,
and it's worthless, like I said. Just an empty buildin' with a
fence around it."

"You have a key to the fence? And the doors?"

"I think so. You want to see 'em?"

"Yeah, I would. Although I don't think they'll do either of us any good."

Lilly stared at him. "Why not?"

"Because," Gunner said, "the locks will have been
changed by now. Unless I miss my guess."

"I'll get 'em for you anyway," Lilly said, shrugging

again, and disappeared into the back of the bar, behind the door marked Employees Only.

Finally, Gunner moved to Little Pete's end of the bar and sat down. "Sorry to keep you waiting, Pete," he said.

The short man lifted his shoulders indifferently. "Anything for a preferred customer. What can I do for you?"

"You can help me make it through the night, partner. It's going to be a long one, I think."

"That right?"

"Yeah."

"How many players you expectin' to see?"

"I don't know. More than the legal limit."

Little Pete pulled a makeshift catalog from one of his pockets and set it on the counter of the bar between them.

"In that case, may I make a few suggestions?" he asked.

"Please do," Gunner said, pulling the catalog closer. "Please do."

13

There was a lookout out front. He was supposed to be just a rummy killing time on the sidewalk, waiting for night to pass into day three steps from the gate of the chain-link fence surrounding the property, but he had shown Gunner more interest than he warranted when the detective made his first pass by the gate to look the place over.

He was a mop-headed, middle-aged man with a pungent aroma and a keen eye, dressed in a tattered pair of dungaree work pants and a polyester shirt with an oversized collar. The bag in his hand had a bottle in it, and the bottle was more than a prop, because he was drunk. Too drunk to be taken for sober, but not drunk enough to miss anything important. He was going to be hard to get past.

Reaching this conclusion himself, approaching the lookout again as his trip around the block came to an end, Gunner decided not to try. The corner of Manchester and Hoover at two in the morning Saturday could not be described as dark, by any means, but the lot that interested the detective was, and traffic along both major boulevards was transient, at best. The gas station on the northeast corner of the intersection was open, but there were no cars at the pumps and the attendant was nowhere to be seen. Performed properly, an open mugging had a good chance of going unnoticed.

Gunner closed upon the tipsy lookout fast and dropped him with a right hand thrown from the hip. A blue Ford showing a strong disregard for the speed limit raced by on the northbound side of Hoover obliviously. Propped up against the chain-link fence, out cold, the lookout struck as unassuming a figure as ever.

Gunner's hunch about Lilly's keys had been right: none of them opened the padlock on the gate. He stopped pushing his luck and went around to the 88th Street side of the lot to jump the fence in relative obscurity.

The former Vons market Lilly had inherited was a vast, boarded-up, graffiti-covered mess, seemingly impossible to penetrate, but one door in the back still looked like a door: it was locked securely by dual padlocks, top and bottom, and was free of any crosshatched wood slats nailed across its face. Gunner shunned any further use of Lilly's keys, undid the tape he had used to tie a stumpy tire iron to his right calf, and went to work on the door, compromising quiet for speed.

It took him a little over six minutes to get inside.

"They're MK760s," Sweet Lou Jenkins said.

He looked tired, but not uneasy. He was trim and fit, dressed to kill even at four in the morning, and his smooth, coffee-colored face seemed totally incapable of projecting distress.

But he *was* distressed.

It seemed to Gunner now that only five minutes had passed, but the reality was that it had been nearly two hours since he had entered the building to learn that somebody was paying the electric bill. The breaker panel he eventually located with the aid of a small flashlight had actually brought some overhead lights on, not that there was much to illuminate: a few rows of empty display cases, a barren freezer box with shattered glass in some of its doors . . .

And seven casket-like wooden crates stacked neatly in the middle of the floor.

Gunner already had two crates open and was setting aside the lid on a third when Sweet Lou made his entrance, Jimmy Price at his right hand, Mouse at his left. Price was wielding a gun.

"Nine millimeters, thirty-six rounds, fully automatic," Jenkins elaborated, stepping forward to take one of the factory-fresh machine guns out of the crate Gunner had just opened. "Navy's big on 'em, I understand."

Gunner watched him fondle the weapon with the awkward touch of a novice and said, "I'm sure the Brothers will be, too."

Price shook his head. "Some niggers just can't be reasoned with," he said, disgusted.

"We should've killed the wise-ass motherfucker when we had the chance," Mouse agreed, moving to pat Gunner down. He found nothing, shook his head at Price and Jenkins, and returned to his position beside the latter.

"You boys forgot your Halloween masks," Gunner said. "Or do I have you confused with somebody else?"

"We called it doing you a favor," Price said. "Disguising ourselves. The plan at the time was to let you live." He shook his head again. "That's not the plan anymore."

"Amen," Mouse said.

Jenkins put the automatic rifle back in the crate and eyed Gunner with grave disapproval. "I'm afraid you've investigated yourself right out of this life, Gunner. It took you a while, but you've finally become more valuable to us dead than alive. And for what? Really?"

"Just the truth," Gunner said succinctly, having no other excuse to fall back on. "For whatever it's worth."

Jenkins grinned. "You think you know the truth?"

Gunner shrugged. "Enough to be dangerous. No pun intended." He nodded toward the crates on the floor. "You're selling guns to the Brothers of Volition. Guns you bought with Lewis Henshaw's money, at a lower price per unit, of course."

"Lewis Henshaw? The White is Right bullshitter running for Congress?" Jenkins laughed. "You think I stole money from that idiot to arm the Brothers of Volition?"

"You didn't have to steal it. Your old college buddy Larry Stewart stole it for you. Or maybe Henshaw donated it willingly, I don't know. I haven't pieced that part together, yet."

"I hope you can do it in the next ten minutes," Price said, smiling. The pistol in his hand was the same chrome-plated Browning automatic he had flashed in Stan Ferris's living room over a week ago.

"I could go on," Gunner said, "but I'd need some help with a few details."

"Such as?" Jenkins asked, amicably.

"Such as why you got involved in this mess to begin with. Why you set it all up."

"Who says I did?"

"I'm giving you credit for having more imagination than Stewart. Maybe I'm wrong."

Jenkins grinned. "Just for fun, let's assume you're not. You're stuck for a motive, is that it?"

"You could say I'm stuck, yeah. Because there had to be more in it for you than the money. I mean, you made a few bucks on the deal, of course. Whatever premium you charged Mayes and the Brothers for the hardware, and anything Stewart or Henshaw may have tossed you for the boost to Henshaw's campaign the Brothers will provide when and if they start flashing this stuff around. But we're talking chump-change for an aristocrat like you. Walking money. You didn't take the risks you have just for that."

"Risks? I took no great risks. I based my play on careful calculation, Gunner, the same as I always do. I went to Roland Mayes and Larry Stewart with separate propositions perfectly suited to the needs and personalities of each. I offered Stewart a chance to lend some credence to his boy Henshaw's ignorant admonitions about the Great Black Menace, and I offered Mayes the opportunity to assume a more literal role in the liberation of our people. No risk there. They could say yes, or they could say no, simple as that. Either way, I had nothing to lose, and everything to gain. Just as I do, even now.

"Because, believe it or not, I am just as tired of being somebody's nigger in the underworld as you or anyone else may be of being one in the so-called straight world. My business is no different from any other in that respect, at least: I can only go so far up the administrative ladder or gain so much of my peers' respect because of what I am, and how I am perceived. Which is why I will very much enjoy seeing Mayes and the Brothers raise some long overdue hell in the house of the Almighty White Man. It's time somebody did. And the irony of a racist white pig like Henshaw footing the bill for the bullets appeals to me more than I can say."

"A pity Buddy couldn't see it the same way," Gunner said.

"Yes. It is a pity. But what happened to Buddy, Buddy brought upon himself, because he couldn't—or wouldn't—find it in his heart to believe my good intentions. He had to second-guess and snoop around, to find things out he was bound to misinterpret. And in the end, he had to be foolish enough to try blackmail."

"Blackmail?" At last, a revelation: Buddy Dorris dabbling in capitalism.

Jenkins was amused by his surprise. "Funny, right? He didn't seem capable. One would think he'd have gone directly to Mayes with the news that Henshaw was subsidizing the Brothers' arsenal and leave it at that. But Stewart showed me the note himself: it was badly misspelled and looked like it had been typed on one of those creaky manuals the Brothers use. Buddy knew how the guns had been paid for and wanted fifty thousand dollars to keep quiet about it. Can you imagine?"

"So you had him killed."

Jenkins shook his head. "I didn't do anything. He was blackmailing Stewart, not me. You think that filthy white boy worked for me?"

"His name was Townsend," Gunner said.

"His name was *shit*! He was a whacked-out faggot that could have blown everything, but Stewart didn't want to dispose of him. He thought he could just pay him off and forget about him. I convinced him otherwise.

"Unfortunately, my good friend Mouse here botched our first shot at the boy, and he went into hiding. We looked around for him, naturally, but we had to be discreet, and that hurt us. We were actually about to give up when you suddenly came on the scene, and then, of course, we got lucky."

"I led you right to him," Gunner said, bitterly.

"Yes. You did, didn't you?"

"What about J.T.? Was he just an accident, or did Townsend have orders to take him and Buddy out together?"

Jenkins smiled. "That was just more good luck. One of life's little coincidences. I was looking for a place to hold the guns the cops couldn't connect me with, and someone mentioned this little gem. You heard I was getting nowhere trying to negotiate with Tennell outright, I suppose."

Gunner nodded.

The grin on Jenkins's face widened. "You're not nearly as stupid as your reputation leads people to believe, are you?"

"No," Gunner said. "Not nearly."

Jenkins began to move about in a small circle, one hand caressing the other thoughtfully. "At another time, in another place, I may have been able to use a hardcase like you, Gunner," he said. "There's something to be said for having so pigheaded a man as yourself on one's side, no matter how misguided or naive. I'm afraid, however, that we've missed our chance to cooperate, you and I. In fact, unless I'm greatly mistaken, I expect our relationship is about to turn quite ugly.

"Because it is obvious to me that you can only know what you do because you have either read, or seen, or actually come into the possession of some form of physical evidence pertaining to my arrangement with Larry Stewart—evidence my associates and I have been trying to locate for some time now. Do you know what I'm referring to?"

"I think so," Gunner said.

"Then you have seen it?"

"Yes."

"And do you know where I might find it?"

"Absolutely."

"Is it in your possession, or does someone else have it?"

"I've got it."

"But not here, of course."

"No. I'm not nearly as stupid as they say, remember?"

"Certainly."

Jenkins stopped his circular pacing for a moment. "Now. The obvious question is forthcoming, I promise you. But before we go any further—I'd like to ask a rather embarrassing one, instead. I hope you won't laugh."

Gunner shrugged again. "It can't be any funnier than Mouse looks with a silk scarf over his head, and I haven't laughed at that, yet. Give it a shot."

Jenkins continued to hesitate, then said, "I'd like to know what it is, exactly, that you have. Photographs, a tape recording, documents of some kind? What?"

"You mean you don't know?"

"No. I have no idea." He was genuinely red-faced. "I only know what it supposedly proves."

Gunner contemplated laughing, but remembered his promise to refrain. "It's a tape," he said, seeing no point in withholding the information. "The video variety. Shot on location in Manhattan Beach, on a street named Agnes Road. Stewart and your boy Price here are the featured performers. The plot's a little thin, but I think it has something to do with twenty-five thousand dollars going from a Lincoln to a BMW."

"He's lying," Price said. His eyes were on Jenkins, and he looked worried.

"You dumb shit," Mouse said. "Buddy followed you!"

"That's not possible," Price said, shaking his head at Jenkins. "I would have noticed something . . ."

"It's those tinted windows," Gunner suggested. "Very hard on the eyes."

"What's done is done," Jenkins said, dismissing the hysteria of his subordinates with a wave of his hand, while masking his own agitation commendably. "Why or how it happened isn't important." He turned to Gunner again. "I presume there's no mistaking the identity of either man?"

Gunner shook his head. "Afraid not. This is a Grade-A piece of cinema."

"Shit," Mouse said.

"In that case, I'll ask that obvious question now, Gunner," Jenkins said gravely. "And I'll only ask it once." He stepped back to give Price a clearer shot at the detective.

"Where is the tape?" Jenkins asked.

Gunner used his head to indicate someone behind Jenkins and said, "*He* has it."

Only Jenkins turned, but that was good enough. His face led Price and Mouse to follow his gaze shortly after.

Jamaal Amir Hill stood only twenty feet away, one of the Navy's beloved MK760s in hand, complete with full magazine. He didn't look like somebody who would have any difficulty, or reservations, about firing it.

"What the fuck you doin' here, Jamaal?" Mouse demanded, his fat man's voice in fine form.

"Put the gun down, Brother Price," Brother Jamaal said, glaring at him. It was as if Mouse had never spoken. "Very carefully please."

"I'd do what he says, Jim," Gunner said. "Nine millimeters, thirty-six rounds, and all that. You'd better tell him again, Lou."

Price suffered a brief moment of indecision, furious, then let the Browning dangle limp from his hand before tossing it to the floor a good distance away. Gunner walked over and picked it up.

"You're makin' a mistake, Jamaal," Mouse said, watching his fellow Brother of Volition move to Gunner's side with the gaze of a crazed animal. "A *big* mistake."

"Shut up, Mouse," Hill said, annoyed.

"So the man has friends," Jenkins said, trying to smile. "How convenient."

"You can zip it too, Lou," Gunner told him, training the Browning on his heart. "Unless you're going to do something predictable like offer me the sun and the moon to let you all go."

Jenkins shook his head effortlessly. "Not that I don't believe you can be bought. I just don't think you're worth owning."

"Here, here," Price said, having a hard time keeping still.

"I suppose you intend to turn us over to the police now?" Jenkins asked.

"In time," Gunner said. "You in a hurry?"

His expression had hardened, grown dark in the shadow of a sudden anger. He turned to Brother Jamaal and said, "Go kill the camera."

Only after Hill stepped behind the broken display case standing several feet before them did the three men see it: the official camcorder of the Brothers of Volition, mounted on its tripod, peering through a forest of carefully placed debris to spy upon them. Hill fingered its controls and a red eye near the lens went black, unceremoniously.

"I've had some trouble lately getting the police to take what I say seriously, so I thought a little visual aid might come in handy," Gunner said. "I hope you gentlemen don't mind."

Finally, Price came at him, as he had been threatening to for some time. Jenkins and Mouse, however, did not move, content for now to watch.

"You take another step and I'm going to have to end this thing a lot faster than I planned to, Price," Gunner told him, pulling the hammer back sharply on the lawyer's chrome Browning, turning its nose to point directly at his chest.

Price froze in midstride at the sound, glared into the black pit of the weapon's barrel, and retreated, reluctantly. His face was a mask of hatred, accented by eyes that said he would try Gunner again, given the chance.

Hill returned to the detective's side and said, "Now what?" Clearly, he, too, was getting edgy.

Gunner reached for the MK760 and swiftly traded the Browning for it, giving Jenkins and the others no time to react before the business end of the automatic rifle was staring back at them again.

"Now we play a game," he said, to no one and everyone, his attention turned to Mouse and Price, exclusively. "Tell him how it's played, Mouse. Or do I have to do it?"

"I don't know what you're talkin' about," the little man said, his eyes on the gun staring him down.

Gunner tipped his head toward the Browning in Brother Jamaal's hand and said, "Empty the clip of all but one round and let him have it. Then give Price the Ruger."

"Gunner. Wait a minute," Jenkins said, uneasily. The man who never lost his cool was suddenly perspiring heavily, ruining his clothes. He seemed to know what was coming.

"Shut up, Lou. You'll get your turn," Gunner said.

"You're not thinking. Jesus, man, what the hell is this going to get you?"

"He's crazy," Price said.

"Goddamn right he's crazy, he thinks I'm gonna play *this* shit," Mouse said, bouncing on the balls of his feet, heady from a runaway adrenaline high. "No way, Gunner. Uh-uh."

"Shut up," Gunner said again, meaning it. Hill was almost finished emptying the Browning's clip.

"All things are negotiable, Gunner," Jenkins said, trying to keep some semblance of dignity in his voice. "A smart man makes money when he holds the upper hand, not enemies. We can work something out, I promise you."

"Get fucked, Jenkins. This is supposed to be fun, the way I remember it. Tell your boss what a kick it is, Price. Tell him what a howling good time you and your little boyfriend here had the last time we all played. Or can't you still see the stupid look on Ferris's face when he realized his gun was empty? I sure as hell can."

Price didn't answer.

"Ready," Brother Jamaal said. He was holding the weapons out for Gunner's inspection, Price's Browning in his right hand, Little Pete's old .38 Ruger Security Six in his left.

"Hand 'em out," Gunner told him.

"What the fuck's wrong with you, Jamaal?" Mouse bellowed, as Hill came toward him. "You're a Brother, man! We only did what we had to do to get Roland and the boys the guns! Can't you see that?"

"I can see you're just as ignorant a fool as I always thought you were," Hill said, passively. "And an even bigger sissy."

"You're going to regret this later, Gunner," Jenkins said, backpedaling casually out of harm's way.

Gunner grinned at him sardonically. "I've had regrets before. One more's not going to kill me."

Mouse had the Browning in his right hand now, down

at his side. He was obviously struggling with the question of what to do with it, and when.

Price, meanwhile, wouldn't take the Ruger from Hill. Roland Mayes's cameraman turned to Gunner, exasperated, and made a face of helplessness.

"Take the gun, Price," Gunner said.

"Fuck you. I'm not your boy." Price laughed. "Let Lou play."

Jenkins whirled, stunned.

"Next round," Gunner said flatly. "Take the gun and spin the wheel. Test your luck. I admit it's not much, but it's a *chance* to get out of here alive. Which is more than you gave Ferris, now isn't it?"

Price studied his face in silence for a long time, defiantly motionless. His rage was like something alive, radiant and withering. When at last he was convinced that Gunner wasn't bluffing, he took the Ruger from Brother Jamaal's grasp, with care and deliberation, and turned to face Mouse squarely, the pistol at his side.

"Don't do it, Jimmy," Mouse said.

Brother Jamaal backed away.

"Thanks for the hand, Jamaal," Gunner said. "You take the tape and get lost now—all right?"

Hill didn't move. "You sure you're going to be okay? If you want—"

Gunner shook his head, said, "Some other time. Just leave the tape where we agreed and go home. I can handle things from here."

Hill went over to the camcorder and retrieved the cassette. He zipped the front of his jacket up over it and started for the door.

"Good luck, brother," he said, and ran off.

When he was sure they were alone, Gunner spoke again. "Game time," he told Price and Mouse.

Mouse started shaking his head, his eyes shut tight.

"That means you, Mouse," Gunner said. The two unwilling duelists were positioned only ten feet away from one another as he held the MK760 steady, ready for any sign of mutiny.

"Either one of you tries anything stupid, I'll cut you both down. In pieces."

"Don't do it, Gunner," Jenkins said, eyeing the investigator imploringly.

"On three," Gunner said, ignoring him. "One."

Mouse still had his eyes closed.

"Two—"

Price's right arm shot up and the Ruger fired once, aimed at Mouse's face. An imperfect hole appeared over the little man's left eye and the back of his head broke up, flesh and bone converted into a small, damp cloud of pink and red. The chrome Browning automatic was still pinned to his side as his body fell, surprise leaving the same mark on his features it had left on Stanley Ferris's.

"Christ," Jenkins said, grimacing.

Price turned smartly on his heels to face Gunner again and threw the spent Ruger to the ground, his face entirely devoid of expression.

"Sorry to jump the gun, hero," he said, "but I trust you feel better now."

Gunner frowned and shook his head, his jaw clamped tight and aching. "Not yet," he said.

The MK760 came alive in his hands and breathed fire, barking with restraint. Price took the blast of nine-millimeter rounds full in the chest and became airborne, like a marionette tossed by its strings. He landed in a heap nearly ten yards away, another corpse ready for burial.

Jenkins stood in mute amazement, staring at the young man's body. He brought his eyes around to Gunner slowly and waited, resigned to the fact that his fate was no longer his own to control.

"Tell me what you saw," Gunner said, calmly.

Jenkins merely shook his head and smiled the thinnest of smiles, ever the cold realist.

"Not a fucking thing," he said.

Just when everyone thought it was safe to abandon the shade, Los Angeles had another record-breaking fall day in the high nineties, but the headline story in all the newspapers was the search for Roland Mayes.

Sweet Lou Jenkins hadn't done much to help, but the LAPD had used Gunner's deposition and video double feature to put together a fairly clear picture of the circumstances surrounding Buddy Dorris's death, and now the only major piece of the puzzle missing was Mayes—Mayes and one case of MK760s that, according to Jenkins, was unaccounted for.

Larry Stewart had confessed to everything, once the state police had pulled him off a late-arriving Delta airliner in Ft. Lauderdale, Florida, fourteen hours after Jenkins's arrest. He had swung some kind of deal with the District Attorney's office involving immunity. It helped Lewis Henshaw some that he had apparently known nothing about his aide's bold attempt to scare up a few thousand more votes for him within the district he was vying to represent, but not much. Rumor had it the Far Right's favorite son was going to spare himself the indignity of being ravaged at the polls by withdrawing his candidacy, and soon.

Gunner, meanwhile, was suspended in an awkward limbo of sorts. The media had built him up to be no less than a hero, the rogue star of a by now famous videotape who had almost single-handedly staved off whatever nameless bloodshed Mayes and the Brothers of Volition would likely have wrought with Jenkins's arsenal, and the police could hardly do anything but agree, at least for the record. But his latest adventure had cost two more lives, and the story he had told this time by way of explanation was flimsier than the last, Jenkins's wholly concurring version notwithstanding. Despite his freedom and Ziggy's encouragement that no new charges against him would be filed, the detective still couldn't decide whether his status had greatly improved or had diminished, and no one within the department—Matt Poole included—was talking.

In Mayes's absence, Jamaal Amir Hill was keeping the lid on the boiling pot that was the Brothers of Volition as best he could, but he seemed to be overmatched. For the moment, their headquarter doors were still open, as no one could prove that anyone but Mayes, Mouse, and Buddy Dorris knew anything about the guns Mayes had made arrangements to buy, or what his plans for their use may or may not have been. But the scrutiny of the world was upon them, and the weight of that much attention was stifling. The police were everywhere, waiting for Mayes to make some kind of contact with his people, and their presence was a constant annoyance. Despite Brother Jamaal's feverish efforts to direct them, to make them recognize how destructive Mayes's intent could have been to their cause in the long run, many Brothers were abandoning ship, breaking off in varied numbers to illustrate their commitment to Mayes, and their tenuous impatience with America's status quo. Some were prepared only to make noise; others were not. These few were ready and hungry for something more, as were millions of others outside their ranks, black men and women nationwide who were following the Brothers' story with keen interest, waiting anxiously to see which way the winds of change were eventually going to blow.

The smoldering flame of racial unrest, only recently believed to be dying with October's oppressive heat, was glowing white hot anew.

Amid all this, little or no attention was paid to Verna Gail. The police questioned her quickly and elected not to hold her, satisfied that she had played no integral part in either the murder of Denny Townsend or the Jenkins-Stewart-Mayes conspiracy. It was possible she knew where Mayes might be hiding, but hardly probable; by all accounts, they were two people who from day one had cared very little for each other. Verna Gail was just a peripheral character in a convoluted plot, the authorities reasoned, a bit player of no significance. So they let her go home and forgot about her. As did Gunner.

For a while.

It took four rings to get her attention, but Verna Gail's voice finally rattled in answer over the intercom system of her apartment building. She sounded half-asleep, but in another five minutes it would be three in the afternoon on a clear-skied Sunday.

"Yes? Who is it?"

Gunner moved closer to the speaker on the wall and in a loud voice identified himself. He wasn't surprised when she took a full minute to answer back.

"Come on in," she said.

Gunner gave the blue, plain-vanilla Ford sedan parked across the street one final look. The plainclothesmen inside appeared to be dozing off. Poole's boys really had lost interest in Verna Gail.

A solenoid buzzed to release the lock on the apartment building's front security door and Gunner stepped inside, only casually noting that the door would have opened regardless: someone had pried it open the hard way and destroyed the jam. He found apartment 104 on the ground level, to the left of the courtyard entrance, but Verna wasn't waiting at the door. He punched the little chime button below the peephole and she finally appeared, looking not a good deal better than she had the day he stumbled upon her rooting through the carnage of her brother Buddy's ransacked apartment. But that was understandable.

Roland Mayes was standing behind her, pressing the lethal end of a sawed-off Remington 1100 twelve-gauge shotgun into the base of her neck.

"Welcome to the party, Cop," he said, grinning. "Glad you could make it."

He motioned Gunner inside and closed the door after him.

Verna's apartment was small and dark, an above-ground bomb shelter insulated from the outside world by drapes drawn tightly together, granting no passage to sunlight. The air conditioner was on, whining evenly. A short, stocky table lamp burned atop a dining-room table near the kitchen, casting odd shadows over three grim-faced black men scattered throughout the living room. They all wore the colors of the Brothers of Volition, as did Mayes, and each had one of Lou Jenkins's familiar MK760s either in hand or nearby, within easy reach. The Brothers' doorman, the big kid with the archaic Afro Gunner had met earlier, was among them, as was one of the giants who had given Mouse a hand in his fistfight with Gunner that same day.

"Brothers, I'd like you to meet Aaron Gunner," Mayes said, seeing Verna to a seat at the end of the couch. She seemed to have no resistance left. "Protector of the innocent and keeper of the peace. Lonnie, you and Marlin remember Gunner, right?"

The big kid with all the hair nodded silently; Mayes

told him to pat Gunner down for weapons, and after a while he crushed out the joint he was smoking and got up from the couch to do so. He slapped the detective around for a while, shook his head at Mayes, and sat back down.

"He's okay," he mumbled.

Mayes looked Gunner over, enjoying himself. "Care to have a seat? Can I get you something to drink?"

Gunner shook his head. "No thanks."

"I hoped you might turn up. In fact, I figured you would. I couldn't see you all of a sudden doing the smart thing, the safe thing, letting sleeping dogs lie. That's not your style."

Gunner grinned. "I guess it isn't."

"How'd you know I'd be here?" Mayes asked.

"I didn't. I came to see the lady."

"Yeah? What for?"

"To ask her a few questions. As you might recall, that's what I do."

Mayes frowned. "Questions? What kind of questions? Your case is closed, Gunner; you've already got all the answers. You know who killed Buddy and you know who killed Townsend. You even know why. What the hell else is there?"

Gunner turned to look at Verna. "There's the matter of the blackmail note that got Buddy killed. And the question of who really wrote it." Verna was watching him now, wild-eyed. "Everybody seems to be satisfied that Buddy did, I know. But I for one have my doubts."

"You too?" Mayes asked, grinning again. His eyes were also on Verna. "What a small world."

"I take it she hasn't 'fessed up, yet."

"No. You take it right. She says I've got it all wrong."

"You do!" Verna snapped, leaping to her feet. "I didn't have anything to do with that note, I swear it!"

"You should have figured it out a lot sooner than I did, Mayes," Gunner said, facing him. "If it seemed strange to me that a man like Buddy would try to hit Stewart and

Jenkins up for fifty thousand dollars, it had to seem twice as funny to you. Buddy didn't give a damn about money, or so everyone said. He would have had no use for blackmail, at least not for profit."

"How the hell would you know?" Verna asked. "You didn't even know him!"

"No, I didn't. But you did. Better than Mayes. Better than anyone. You were his big sister; his confidante. The one person he could go to with problems too big to share with anyone else. Like what to do with the knowledge that the guns Mayes and the Brothers were buying from Sweet Lou Jenkins, the very same guns most of our friends here are sporting, had been paid for out of Lewis Henshaw's pocket."

"No!"

"Shut up, Verna!" Mayes said. "Let the man finish."

"The man *is* finished," Gunner said. "Buddy asked for his sister's advice and got it, only it wasn't what a proletarian in good standing like Buddy wanted to hear. So the lady decided to turn the screws on Larry Stewart herself, without Buddy's knowledge, and without the benefit of knowing what kind of specific proof Buddy had of Stewart's deal with Jenkins. I think Buddy told her everything but that."

"Which would explain why the blackmail note never actually mentioned Buddy's videotape," Mayes said.

Gunner nodded. He said to Verna, "The day I found you at your brother's apartment, you were cleaning up the mess *you'd* made the night before. Weren't you?"

"Bullshit," Verna said.

"You were looking for Buddy's proof, because without it you had nothing to back up the note with. But you didn't know what you were looking for, and you found that somewhat frustrating. So you trashed the place."

"No!"

"Stop lying, goddammit!" It was Mayes. He had the Remington aimed in the vicinity of her lower torso, and his face was contorted with rage. "The cop's right, and we all know it! Buddy didn't write that fucking blackmail note, *you* did!"

He turned to Gunner and said, "Buddy brought the news of the tape to me, thinking it would change my mind about the guns. Only it didn't, of course. I didn't give a damn where Jenkins was getting the money for the stuff, and I told Buddy that. If Henshaw was involved, so what? He had no control over what we were going to do with the hardware, and neither did anyone else. That, to me, was all that mattered.

"But it mattered to Buddy. He was as ready as any of us for guerrilla warfare, but he was afraid something would backfire, that the Brothers would get hurt somehow if I went through with the deal. He said he'd go public with what he knew if I didn't call it off. But I managed to change his mind. I convinced him to wait, to trust me. To give my leadership a chance to show dividends. Because Buddy *was* my brother, and I was his, no matter what many people thought. I had everything under control.

"And then Stewart got his note. And a few days after that, Buddy was dead."

Mayes smiled, painfully. "Those bastards never even gave me a chance to talk to him."

He returned his gaze to Verna and closed upon her, lifting her chin deftly with the Remington's stout barrel. "But I know what he would have said, all the same," he said. "He would have said I was crazy. That he hadn't sent Stewart any blackmail note and he didn't know who had. Isn't that right, Verna?"

He nudged the shotgun harder into the flesh of her throat, and waited. Almost imperceptibly, she nodded her head, tears rolling quietly down her face.

"I thought I could make something good happen for both of us," she said, her voice broken and all but inaudible. "We never had a dime to spare our whole lives, Buddy and me. And I was tired of it, even if Buddy wasn't. I thought it would be easy.

"Only the fuckers didn't pay." Her eyes began to smolder with new life, hot coals glowing red with regret for the nightmare her plan had become. "They killed Buddy instead. So I looked for the tape, just like you said. But not because I thought it could still get me anything—I didn't care about the money anymore. I just wanted to see Stewart and Sweet Lou squirm when the cops nailed them with it. The two of them nailed to the cross—that's what I wanted to see."

She shook her head wildly, crying again. "But I didn't know what I was looking for! I didn't *know*!"

She broke down completely, burying her face in her hands. Unmoved, Mayes shoved her back down on the couch, laughing maniacally.

"You're right, Cop," he said to Gunner. "I *should* have figured it out a lot sooner. But better late than never, huh?"

His friends laughed, too, not wanting to miss out on the fun. The fat man Gunner didn't recognize and the giant Gunner did slapped their right hands together, standing behind the couch. Gunner only now took note of the large ice chest sitting on top of the coffee table at the center of the room.

"What is all this anyway, Mayes?" he asked. "A picnic?"

The Brothers saw him eyeing the ice chest and cracked up again, privy to some inside joke. Mayes grinned and said, "Yeah. A picnic. Like the one the Texans had at the Alamo." He moved to the cooler and gingerly pulled off the lid. "Come take a look."

Gunner obliged, and immediately regretted it. Inside the insulated chest, several pounds of incendiary explosives lay submerged in a clear, yellowish liquid whose odor betrayed the fact that it was kerosene. It was a crude combination that constituted a bomb big enough to level the building they were all standing in and a few others to either side, and Gunner didn't have to be a demolitions expert to know it.

"Seeing as how we owe you for Brother M.," Mayes said, "welcome to Roland Mayes's last stand." He grinned again, proudly.

"Jesus Christ," Gunner said, in stunned disbelief. "You have any idea how many innocent people you're liable to kill with this shit?"

"I'm not interested in lives lost," Mayes said. "I'm interested in lives saved. It's the future I'm concerned with now, Gunner. Not the present or the past. We're going to make history here today, you, my friends, and I. We're going to light up the new Big Bang, and change the goddamn universe!"

"Right on," the kid named Lonnie said.

Mayes went to the living-room window and gestured for Gunner to follow. He took a pair of binoculars from the Brother nearest the window and held the edge of the curtains back so that Gunner might peek out.

"Take a good hard look at the men in that blue Ford across the street," he said.

It was the same car Gunner had noticed earlier, only now he could see that the clean-cut plainclothes officers in the front seat had not merely dozed off on the job. They were dead, each shot once in the head at close range.

"As you can see, Brother Marlin does excellent work," Mayes said, as Gunner handed back the binoculars. "They've been sitting like that for over forty minutes now—which means they'll well overdue to be missed. Only one car will come to check on them at first, but that will soon be followed by many, many others. And what will happen then, Cop? Care to guess?"

"A firefight," Gunner said, suddenly wishing Lilly were around to pour him a stiff drink. "And a big one."

Mayes nodded. "Exactly. The Man will go off in all his righteous, indignant glory. While the world watches, the paramilitary puppets of the established order will cut this building to ribbons, and one bullet or another, either one of ours or one of theirs, will hit that chest. And my work on this earth will be done."

"You're crazy," Gunner said.

Mayes lay the Remington's muzzle against the detective's chest, lazily. "How so?" he asked.

"You're crazy to try it. And even crazier to think it'll change a goddamn thing. That's how so."

"You're wrong," Mayes said. "The time is right. Our people are ready for this moment. How many more great thinkers and leaders do you think our brothers and sisters will watch the White Man cut down before they finally take to the streets? Five? Ten? A hundred?" Mayes shook his head. "No. Not now. Not ever again. I'm betting my life the buck's going to stop *here*."

"And when our brothers and sisters take to the streets? What then? What will they have bought in the lousy three or four days of warfare they'll be capable of waging against a multibillion-dollar system of government primed to turn them back? A little more respect? A little more recognition?"

"They'll have a start. And that's better than the nothing they've had up to now, isn't it?"

"A start to what? To where? We've spent a hundred and fifty years trying to prove to the White Man that we can handle civilization just as easily as he can, and you want to wipe that out in a week. I don't get it."

"You don't have to get it," Mayes said angrily. "All you need to 'get' is that I'm tired of trying to force social reform on a race of people rendered by the system too ignorant to comprehend my message. Buddy was right; blood must be spilled. And so I'm through talking. I'm through listening. And so are you." He used the shotgun in his hands to point at a lounge chair facing the couch, near the coffee table. "Go sit down, Cop," he said.

Gunner gazed into the large, almond-shaped eyes staring him down and saw madness, unabated. He went to the chair and sat down, without argument.

"Guess you should have left well enough alone," Verna said, smiling at him, her eyes damp and glistening.

Gunner didn't answer her. He was too preoccupied with the business of deciding whether the next several minutes of his life would be better spent preparing himself for the hereafter, or designing a way to survive. The first would be difficult; the second, nearly impossible. Four sets of eyes were intermittently upon him and there was nothing within his reach that would fare well against either the twelve-gauge rounds of Mayes's Remington or the nine-millimeter casings of his friends' MK760s. Whatever he tried now would fail, and fail miserably. He had to wait for an opening, and hope he would know what to do with it when it came. *If* it came.

Before the police did.

The fuzz-headed kid named Lonnie was lighting a fresh joint. His automatic rifle was in his lap, but he had it turned so that Gunner could look down its barrel, just to remind the detective it was there. It was clear that he had a buzz on, but not so clear how much of one; he still seemed to have a firm command of all his faculties.

A siren started to sound in the distance. The cavalry was on its way.

The fat man and the giant went to the window to join Mayes, the three of them peeling back the curtain to look out. Lonnie looked up once, then turned his eyes on Gunner and kept them there. Verna didn't move.

"This is it. Get ready," Mayes told the two at the window. They nodded their heads solemnly and disappeared into the bedroom, taking their weapons with them. Mayes tossed a cursory glance at the others and returned his attention to the street outside.

"You'd better cover that up," Gunner said to the kid on the couch, pointing at the open ice chest filled with kerosene. "Either that, or put that fucking roach out."

There was a slight pause as the man with the oversized Afro pondered the suggestion. He didn't like being told what to do, but finally got up and reached for the lid, the glowing marijuana joint wedged between two fingers on his right hand.

It wasn't the low-risk play Gunner had wanted to make, but it was the best he could come up with. He reached out with his right foot and kicked the cooler once, hard, splashing kerosene over the edge. A length of Lonnie's right arm and the front of his shirt went dark with the liquid for only a split second, then burst into flame as the cigarette in his hand ignited, creating a human torch. The big man fell away from the coffee table before the chest itself could ignite and dropped the rifle in his other hand to fight the fire, screaming in agony, his eyes a testament to abject horror.

As Verna's own screams joined Lonnie's, Mayes whirled away from the window, but too late: Gunner's newfound MK760 raced the sawed-off Remington into position and won, spraying a haphazard nine-millimeter line of fire that brought the head Brother of Volition to his knees, clutching at two wounds in his upper body. The two men in the other room appeared at the bedroom door immediately after, only to run headlong into a hail of bullets they never had time to answer. They fell one on top of the other, face down in the carpet, and were still.

Gunner looked around for Verna and just caught a glimpse of her as she ran out the front door. To where, he couldn't imagine. The wail of the onrushing siren was almost deafening now. She wasn't going to get far.

And neither was Mayes, though he was still alive. He was sitting on the floor with his back against the wall and his legs stretched out in front of him, watching in a daze as the kid named Lonnie smothered the last of the flames burning his right arm with his blackened, shredded shirt. Most of the right side of the kid's upper torso was black, as well, and he looked to be in shock, no threat to anyone anywhere, soon.

"Let it go, Brother Mayes," Gunner said, wearily.

The sawed-off Remington lay on the floor not far from the head Brother's right hand, and despite the pair of leaking holes in his chest, Mayes was trying to find the strength to reclaim it. Outside, the police siren had stopped, and now the two men could hear the sounds of frantic activity in the street, doors slamming closed and radios sizzling with static.

Mayes's hand moved closer to the gun, his eyes on the cooler atop the coffee table.

"You blow that ice chest now, and you'll make history, all right," Gunner said, pulling the bolt back on the automatic rifle he was holding for emphasis. "They'll call you the biggest black American *fuck-up* ever born."

Gunner said nothing more. He just let Mayes make up his own mind.

Because that was the least he could do, for a brother.

15

It turned out that Roland Mayes was unwilling to settle for infamy over fame. For all his altruism, he still had a certain fondness for himself and his place in history.

The great war between the races he had originally hoped to lead never took place. His well-publicized arrest and subsequent imprisonment were catalysts to a number of minor, unrelated incidents of protest nationwide, inevitably, but millions of heads did not roll and blood did not flow freely in the streets. White America, it seemed, had survived yet another threat to its stranglehold on the destiny of Black America, and Black America, at least until the next Roland Mayes came along, had resigned itself once again to wait, to persevere, to keep the dream alive that the system that continued to work against it would someday heal itself.

But the Brothers of Volition episode did not come and go without making some valuable impact, however minor, on the lives of several principals involved. If nothing else more substantial had been accomplished, Lilly Tennell had slowly learned to own and operate the Acey Deuce without her husband's assistance; Mean Sheila Pulliam had discovered the hard way that you don't make a racket when ambushing a man from behind; Terry Allison was shown that a dinner date with a given black man could be as thought-provoking and stimulating as one with a given man of any other race, color, or creed.

And Aaron Gunner finally figured out what it was he wanted to be for the rest of his wretched life.

Which is why he went out of his way one Tuesday afternoon in late November to catch up with an old friend, a man with a motor-mouth and a heart of tarnished gold. His search started and ended in Will Rogers park in Watts, on a hard wooden bench near the basketball courts and a drinking fountain that didn't work. The friend was sitting there in ragged clothes, his skin as dark as the leather of his shoes, an old fishing cap atop his gray head. There was a bottle in a paper sack in his left hand.

"What's happening, Too Sweet?" Gunner asked, sitting down beside him.

Too Sweet Penny grinned a toothless grin. "How you been, Gunner, my man? I seen you on TV, you know that? On the six o'clock news, I think it was."

"Yeah. That was me."

"They talkin' 'bout givin' you your license back, huh?"

Gunner shrugged. "They're talking, yeah."

"Shit, they got to give it back! You a goddamn hero, you know that? I was tellin' a boy over here just the other day, I know that boy, Aaron Gunner. Best goddamn private investigator you can buy, I said! I tell everybody that, man."

"I know, Sweet. That's why I'm here."

Gunner pulled a fifty-dollar bill out of his wallet and stuffed it in the old man's right hand.

"Keep up the good work," he said.

For the next twenty minutes, Too Sweet thanked him profusely, even though Gunner had only stuck around for the first five.